Kenzie -

I love you

always!

♥ AMY

Doolittle

DOOLITTLE

By Amy Morris-Young
With George Howard

ISBN: 9798392697601
Imprint: Independently published

This book is a work of fiction. References to real people, events, establishments, organizations, or locales are provided only to add a sense of authenticity. All other characters, incidents and dialogue are drawn from the authors imagination and are to be construed as fiction.

First publication date: May, 2023

Doolittle

About the Authors

Amy Morris-Young

Amy Morris-Young was born and raised in the Los Angeles, California area, but has lived in Washington state for 35 years, and considers herself a Pacific Northwest "local." She taught writing at Loyola Marymount University in Los Angeles, is known for her national "Notes from Nonna" columns, and her work has been included in multiple anthologies, including *The Way of Kindness*. Amy and her husband Dan have a combined family of six children and eight grandchildren; she enjoys cooking for all of them, and hearing little kids giggle at the movies.

George Howard

George Howard was born in Aberdeen, Washington, in 1930. He is a graduate of Grays Harbor Community College in Aberdeen as well as El Camino College in Torrance, California. George had a long and productive career in aerospace, research and engineering, including working for Northrop, Hughes Aircraft and Honeywell in California. George and his wife Shirley raised four children in Bellevue, Washington, before moving to Lopez Island and then Coupeville, before Shirley's death in 2001. George has nine grandchildren and 13 great grandchildren, and enjoys Dixieland Jazz and Mariners baseball.

Doolittle

Chapter 1 – Doc

David "Doc" Doolittle was born in Aberdeen, Washington, on Valentine's Day, 1960. His father Ben worked at the Grays Harbor paper mill most of his life, after he got out of high school until the mill closed down in 1992. David's mother Lena taught fourth grade at Stevens Elementary School, on the poor side of the Chehalis River.

Ben often called Lena 'one smart cookie,' and bragged that she could have taught at Grays Harbor College just down the road. But Lena just as often replied that by the time her students got to that age it was 'too late.' She said she liked to try to catch them young, when they 'still had a little hope.'

David got his nickname at Stevens Elementary. When he was seven years old, the movie version of the book *Doctor Dolittle* came out, starring Rex Harrison and Anthony Newley. When his mom took him to a Saturday Matinee at the old Gaumont Theatre on Union Street, he remembers smiling over his popcorn as the British man talked to animals, and tapping his foot to the jaunty tunes. He never imagined that just two days later, when he walked into his second-grade classroom, his name would change forever.

Big Sven Sather was the first one to yell, "Hey, Doctor Doolittle!" as David hung up his coat on the hook in his cubby. By recess, all the boys in his class were calling David 'The Doctor.'

David wanted to correct them, to remind them that his name was spelled with two Os, not one. But he knew it had already happened. One of his dad's many sayings was: 'Some things are in your future, some are already in your past.'

So, David just put his hands in his pockets and looked down at the gravel playground. At seven, he was already adept at picking his battles. He daily negotiated the no-win position of having his mom working as a teacher at his school. And since first grade--when he had gotten his first pair of glasses--he had dealt with the extra side bonus of being taunted for having 'four eyes.'

He was way too smart to even try to argue with Big Sven, so-called because he was almost as tall as most of their fathers. He had been held back a couple of grades, a couple of times. David was pretty sure that by the time the last school bell rang, Sven had the start of a five-o'clock shadow.

After a while, the kids at school went from calling him 'The Doctor' to just 'Doc.' And that's what everybody called him until he graduated from J. M. Weatherwax High School. Even his dad called him Doc, since most of his classmates' dads also worked at the mill. Only his mom still called him David, and when he was busted, David Valentine Doolittle.

Doolittle may have known enough not to stand up to bullies like Big Sven, but he still watched them all carefully, noting the dynamics of how they managed their packs of lesser bullies, toadies, flunkies and victims. Whenever he felt the threat of those scraggly gangs nearing him, Doolittle usually managed to sidestep it somehow. He could see trouble coming from a long way off. He secretly believed that was one of his superpowers.

In 1978, most of his fellow male graduates automatically got jobs at the mill, and a few others went into the military. Aberdeen didn't send too many kids to college. But his mom had a thing or two to say about that.

So, Doolittle earned his AA from Gray's Harbor College, then transferred to the University of Washington up in Seattle. At 'U-Dub,' he ended up majoring in Criminology, which seemed to flow logically from his superpower: to watch behaviors of bullies, sort out their crew's pecking orders, and second-guess their next moves.

His mom attended his UW graduation, and he took her out to a nice fish dinner at Duke's Bar and Grill at the base of Queen Anne Hill. His mom had smiled as she looked up at the Space Needle, only a couple blocks away. It was a good night for them both. His dad didn't make it; he had to work a shift at the mill.

With his Criminology degree, he was summarily accepted at the Police Academy in Burien, right under the flight path of SeaTac Airport. Again, going there seemed his next logical step.

On the first day, he saw Barbara Vance—one of only three women in that class--walking across the quad. He felt his feet follow her and the gal with whom she was chatting. His brain seemed to have no choice. He would later say that he "chased Barbara until she caught him."

They graduated together, but unlike her, he did not accept his commission as a police officer. He resented the chain of command; it reminded him too much of the power politics of Big Sven and his cronies. So, he found a beat-up office in Georgetown--in the industrial south end of Seattle--and had gold letters painted onto the glass front door: 'Private Investigator.'

His academy buddy Sam Choi, who still lived with his folks in the International District, also backed away from becoming a cop. Guys at the academy nick-named him Sam Chink. This was not only about the nicest thing they called him, it also irritated the hell out of him, since Sam was Korean, not Chinese.

That systemic ignorance and bigotry in the ranks of the Seattle Police Department was enough to compel Sam say yes to Doolittle's request to join him as a partner. A gold letter S was added to the office door, which now read: 'Private Investigators.'

Sam had an easy commute to their Georgetown storefront office. It was a straight shot from his parents' apartment around the corner from Uwajimaya's Asian Grocery Store by Union Station at 5th and Weller.

On her starting salary as a cop, plus his meager earnings, Barbara and Doc were able to buy a tiny one bedroom, one bathroom house in Ballard. From their front room window, they could see the tourists lining up to watch salmon climb the fish ladders at the Lake Union locks.

It was a rough neighborhood then. Rows of graying worn houses mostly inhabited with graying worn people. But his old Buick seemed at home in the carport, and he could drop Barbara at her precinct on his way to the office, then pick her up on his way home. That worked just fine since they couldn't afford a second car anyway.

He watched as Barbara's feet barely seemed to touch the sidewalk of her beat on Capitol Hill. A smart, attractive, female officer, she ticked all the boxes to be fast-tracked into management. Within a year, she was assigned to an office at the Seattle Police Department Headquarters on 5th Avenue between Cherry and James, right next to the I-5 freeway at the base of Hospital Hill. She worked as the liaison between the SPD and the Mayor's office. He still could have dropped her off on his way to Georgetown, but now she could afford to buy her own car.

She worked hard, and moved up quickly. To match her nice car, she bought nice suits, which made it into countless black and white photos of her and the police mucky-mucks on the pages of the Seattle Times and Post Intelligencer.

But for all that hoopla, Barbara still cooked him dinner most nights and they talked about the characters at their jobs and their frustrating days, and made love a lot. He never could quite figure out why this amazing woman had said 'yes' when he asked her to marry him. She was an extraordinary woman and he was just an ordinary guy.

Doolittle considered his ordinariness another of his superpowers. He thought of himself as solidly average. Average height: 5'9." Average build, average face, dark framed glasses, mid-color everything from his hair to his clothes to the used Buick Regal sedan he drove. He often reassured his clients that he "could get lost in a crowd of two or more people."

When you are in the business of watching people, being invisible comes in handy.

Another of his strengths was that he never got bored. Even as a kid, he just really didn't understand it when other kids said they were bored. There was always something to think about. He could sit in his Buick for hours, sipping coffee, just looking at a building or staring into space, thinking. And waiting.

As time went on, he and Sam divvied up the chores of the business--and the chunks of the days and nights-- seemingly organically. They never really discussed it, it just happened. Sam was good with the office, greeting the customers, handling the paperwork, hunting out documents at the courthouse and the county and the library. Plus Mrs. Choi wanted him home every night by 6pm for her amazing steaming suppers. His growing belly was proof that he was only too happy to oblige her.

Doolittle just as naturally took on all the night shifts. He could wander into a bar or restaurant, nurse a beer and trade small talk with the bartender for hours, then casually trail a customer--or more often a couple of them--back to their car, hotel, apartment, house. His ordinariness made him just another forgettable guy at the bar. His hunched figure melded into the shadows in his parked car, until the movement of his targets quietly triggered his camera to come up and turn their furtive actions into history.

The services of Doolittle and Choi Private Investigators were somewhat pricey, but worth it. They were non-descript, discreet and most often gleaned results. They never bought advertising. Former clients' word of mouth sent them plenty of customers. Husbands concerned about their wives. Wives mistrusting their husbands. Business partners needing assurance about their counterparts. Once in a while even cops or lawyers requiring a work-around the standard justice system.

Doolittle and Sam's partnership was as dependable and unchanging as it was successful. Neither of them big-spenders, they both put a lot of money into their respective bank accounts. Sam bought Mr. and Mrs. Choi a lovely house in West Seattle, above Alki Beach, with a sparkling view across the water of the Seattle skyline.

Barbara and Doc's house value steadily appreciated with the neighborhood around them. They never moved, because as time went on, they were basically only there to eat, sleep, shower, and dress, each one usually alone. Barbara had more and more commitments after hours, and their evenings together dwindled as her career prospects increased.

She occupied the house from after work until the morning. Doc arrived from his dark night shifts usually a bit after sunrise. In the summers, when the sun rose early, he might catch Barbara at home, share some eggs, trade some gossip. In the winters, he generally arrived too late, to an already empty house.

Doolittle told himself that it was probably better that they never had kids. Barbara was now in the highest echelons of Seattle law enforcement. And his and Sam's business was solid, reliable, predictable. The names of their clients and the faces of the people they followed or checked into might change, but the secret liaisons, shady embezzlements, and crooked contracts seemed to be pretty much the same. People were people. There didn't seem to be many new twists.

That's probably why he felt so surprised this particular morning. After he pulled the Buick into their carport, and put his key into the side door, he realized he didn't have to squint and fumble in the darkness as he usually did. The doorknob was brightly lit from behind the gauzy kitchen window curtain.

As he pushed open the door, Barbara looked up from the kitchen table. His heart flipped a bit in his chest, as it always did when he saw her. They had been married for twenty years. Her face had a few lines, and her hair was slightly graying above her ears and at her forehead, but her eyes were big and gray and intelligent, she had a fine straight figure. As he did every single time he laid eyes on her, he wondered how he was so lucky to have this handsome woman for his wife.

But his smile disappeared when he saw the look on her face. Something was different. Something was wrong.

"Barb," he said, laying his briefcase and thermos down on the kitchen counter next to the door. "Good morning."

She raised her chin slightly in answer. He caught a sad look in her eyes, as she glanced down at her hands on the table, then back up at him.

His heart thumped again, but not in a good way. There was a resolve in her look. He tried to sound casual, "Hey, what's going on?"

Barb swallowed, and her fingers splayed on the table. He could feel it, before it came out of her mouth. He watched her face as she talked, the words registering even though it was through a hazy filter. Shimmering sections of the chimera included overlapping veils of his deep love for and admiration of her. Acceptance of the steady morphing of their passion into friendship and then into just being housemates on different sides of the clock. Reluctance to admit the need to acknowledge that and actually make a change. To their routines. To their marriage. To their lives.

When she said the word 'divorce,' he felt himself snap out of the spell of the backlit patina that was like an aura around her beautiful face.

When she was done talking, he heard himself reply, "Yeah. Yeah, I see that." He inhaled deeply, then sighed out the breath. It felt heavy on the way out; it left him empty. But there was nothing to say, really. Barbara was smart, she was kind, she was fair, and of course, she was right.

"Okay then," he said. He pulled back a chair from the table, and sat down, already defeated. Somehow, the ending of their marriage had already happened. Some things are in your future, some already in your past. He realized it must have been a dead thing for a long time. Now, all they had to do was plan its funeral. Silent, he looked at Barbara. And listened to her plan.

It was a good plan. Fair. Barbara had already found a condo in North Seattle, not far from UW and Children's Hospital. Their house was worth a lot of money now, more than a million dollars. They would sell it, split the money, and not be married anymore.

He nodded. It all made sense. Of course it did. He realized he just felt very tired now. This had happened, it was done. Now he could only think that he had been up all night, and the caffeine from his thermos of coffee had been worn off hard by this conversation. The kitchen light felt too bright, and hurt his eyes. He just needed to sleep.

Doolittle

Chapter 2 – Lena

The only part of Barbara's plan that Doolittle hadn't followed was his buying a condo. He just couldn't get his head around dealing with some Condominium Owners Association. He had dealt with enough of those in his profession to believe that they were anything but groups of back-stabbing gossips, most often led by big fish in their little ponds, bullies that reminded him too much of Big Sven.

So instead of investing his half of the house sale in some partially-owned box in a building, he phoned the landlord to whom he and Sam paid rent for their office space. Doolittle had remembered that there was a small utility apartment somewhere upstairs, above the warehouse section of the building, towards the back near the train tracks.

Sure enough, the unit was empty, and for a few hundred bucks every month, he had the smallest work commute in the greater Seattle area: down two sets of stairs and a short walk from the back of the building to their front door.

He banked his half of the proceeds from the house sale, as well as most of his income. It really didn't matter much to him. Life went on, and his needs were few. He worked nights, ate his main meal at breakfast at the diner catty-corner across from the office on Carleton Avenue. He slept, showered, dressed and then did it all again. His only nod to progress was trading his old used Buick for a newer used Buick.

He found himself taking long walks along the water at Lincoln Park on his days off, skimming the occasional flat rock and watching the Fauntleroy Ferry coming and going.

Sam's mother had her match-making friends find Sam a nice girl. He was happy to discover that Lisa was also a smart, funny and very nice-looking lady. They married and he bought a second house in West Seattle, a couple blocks south from his folks. It was conveniently close to his mother's nightly dinners, much to Lisa's relief, as she was a terrific accountant but a miserable cook.

After dinner, Lisa would help wash the dishes, then head home. Sam would stay a while longer, ostensibly to further his cribbage rivalry with his father, but really it was to give his tiny brittle mom a break, and help his nearly blind dad get himself ready for bed.

As they do, the years flipped by. Traffic would swell between T-Mobile Park and the office during the Seattle Mariners' season every April through September. Then it would congest again during the winters due to the Seattle Seahawks' games at Quest Field. Christmas would come up fast, and then it was a new year again. Somehow, twenty years were behind them.

Sam's father had died first, and then his mom went soon afterwards. Sam and Lisa had moved into his parents' house--for the dinner smells in the walls, the cribbage memories and the water view--and rented out their other house.

They had married too late to have kids, so once Sam's folks were gone and their nights were long, they rescued a yappy, smelly, snuggly pug they named Kimchee. He had an ugly smashed face, an underbite, and his greasy rolls stunk like rank dog sweat. They adored him and spoiled him rotten. As Kimchee aged, so did their tender care of him. Sam and Lisa often talked about retirement, but neither had done much about that yet. They were happy and set in their ways.

Doolittle's life moved along just as predictably, adjacent to theirs.

Everything was just fine for him until the morning of Barbara's wedding. It was a beautiful sunny Saturday—a nice surprise of sunshine in early May--and he really did intend to go. He held the invitation in one hand, and his tie in the other. He looked in the mirror, and then he heard and felt a sudden snap.

Snap. He stared at his face. His ordinary face with glasses. His blue eyes and still mostly brown hair. His softer middle, but still strong chest, arms, legs.

Snap. He let the invitation and the tie drop at the same time. They both fluttered to the floor, landing in silence. *You're 62 years old*, he thought. *What the hell are you doing?*

Doolittle did not attend the wedding.

On Monday morning, when Doolittle walked through their office door, Sam looked up from his desk.

Doolittle stopped midway between the door and the desk and announced, "I'm done, Sam."

Sam just tilted his head slightly and pushed his glasses back on his nose. "With what?"

Doolittle waved both arms outwards, encompassing the office space. "This." Then he motioned upwards, towards the back of the building where his apartment was. "And that. All of this."

Sam put his pen down, and took off his glasses. "Okay, Doc. Talk to me. What's up?"

While Sam breathed on the lenses, rubbed them with the bottom of his shirt, and put them back on, Doolittle pulled out the chair in front of Sam's desk and sat down.

He put his hands on his knees and looked at his partner. "Like I said, Sam. I'm all done. I am outa here."

Sam remained still, and just blinked through his glasses.

Doolittle pulled a packet of papers from his inside jacket pocket and tossed them onto the desktop in front of Sam. "I bought this yesterday."

Sam opened up the tri-folded paperwork, and read out loud: "Class C RV. Jayco Redhawk. Chevy Silverado 1500 chassis..." his voice trailed off, and he looked up. "So?"

Doolittle stood up, put his left hand on his hip and thumbed over his right shoulder towards the door, "She's out there. I'm calling her Lena."

Sam muttered, "After your mom." He craned his neck to look around Doolittle's left hip, and was just able to see the royal blue front end of a pickup truck with a camper shell on it. He looked up at him, "Lena. Okay. And?"

"That's my new home, Sam. This," Doolittle gestured around the office again, "This is all yours, if you want it. I'm outa here. Today."

Sam still looked perplexed, but nodded as he processed the information. "Well, okay then, Doc. I'm sure we can work something out. How long do you think you'll be gone? I mean, I can hire a temp to cover some office stuff, take care of some of the night stuff myself, and…"

Doolittle cut him off, "Forever. I'm gone forever, Sam. This is it for me."

Sam stopped talking, and his eyes widened behind his glasses.

Doolittle continued, "I spent the morning settling stuff. Paid off the apartment through the end of the month. Moved the few things I want to keep into Lena. When my Social Security checks start coming , they will get automatically deposited in my checking account, so I can access that from anywhere. Plus, you know we really don't have to worry about money, Sam." Doolittle smiled lopsidedly, one side of his face pulling into a deep dimple, "We did good here, man. You and me. I thank you, Sam."

Sam nudged his chair backwards and stood up. He faced his partner over the desk, searching his eyes. "You are serious about this." It wasn't a question. He had known Doc since the Academy, had worked with him all of his adult life. He had only seen him this determined a handful of times. Doolittle was not a gray area sort of guy. He was black and white, and this decision appeared to have the ink already drying on it.

"Well. Okay, Doc. We'll sort the money thing out then, I guess. Draw it up. Um, where do you want me to send any paperwork?"

Doolittle laid a piece of paper on the desk. "My folks' house in Aberdeen. There's a renter in there now, but it's some sort of second cousin of my mom. I can pick up mail there until I get a PO Box somewhere. I'll let you know where, or if, I land, okay?"

Sam nodded and stuck out his right hand.

"Okay. Well. I'm not going to say goodbye, because you are stuck with me, man. I am right here for you, always. But I will say good luck."

Doolittle grabbed Sam's hand, shook it firmly, then Sam's hands dropped to his sides.

"I know that, Sam. Thanks. And same, same. If you need me, call. I'm taking my same cell phone with me. Don't know where I'll be, or how long it will take me to get here, but you know I'll come."

Sam rubbed one eye behind his glasses. He cleared his throat. "Okay then?"

"Yep," Doolittle turned and walked to the door. He looked back, "Okay then."

When he closed the office door behind him--making the front buzzer sound--Sam stood there staring for a few moments, then he sat down hard. He shook his head, as if to make all the bits of new information and thoughts settle into their new pockets in his brain. Then he reached for the desk phone to call his wife.

Doolittle climbed into the cab. He didn't look back at the office. He had seen that storefront maybe thousands of times.   No way would he ever forget what those Doolittle and Choi gold letters on the glass door looked like.

He looked into his side mirror, then over his left shoulder and pulled away from the curb, merging into the traffic on Carleton Avenue. The south onramp to the I-5 freeway was straight ahead, and he took it.

Funny thing about driving, he thought, as the truck moved along with the rest of the southbound traffic. *It's mostly your body, not your brain. I could almost do this in my sleep.* He smiled, *But I guess I better not.*

He ticked off the names on the signs that he had lived by--mostly seen at night—which were like conduits into the all the towns and neighborhoods where he had trailed, surveilled, and documented people's actions, turning them into evidence and a paycheck.

Tukwila, SeaTac, Federal Way, Fife, Tacoma. When he saw Joint Base Lewis McCord coming up on the left, he took the Dupont exit on the right. He fueled the truck at the 76 station at the roundabout, and got the free hot dog that came with it. He paid cash. An old habit. Something about staying invisible.

When he passed Olympia, he saw the signs for ocean beaches, Highway 101, Aberdeen. Doolittle didn't know exactly why he was getting pulled back to the coast. He had clambered over every inch of those sand dunes and grass and gravel as a kid. *Mom and dad are long gone.*

What is there left to see? he wondered. He shrugged and kept going.

The truck kept right, arcing smoothly onto the 101 north, then he kept left at the Y onto State Route 8 towards Aberdeen. That turned into Highway 12 at Elma. He hadn't driven this in years, but these were well-worn grooves, and there was comfort in that, a dimming of his old life, of just being in the present.

Going home, he thought. Then he raised his chin with remembering. *Oh yeah. I'm bringing my home with me.* He felt how the weight of the camper sat on the truck, how it lugged down the speed and kept him in the slow lane. He smiled. *I've got my house on my back, like a turtle.*

At Montesano, he briefly considered taking the 107 south. It looped back into Hwy 12 and was a pretty drive. He shook that idea off and stayed the course. When he passed Junction City, he started to feel memories bunch up in his shoulders and chest. *There's the water, the sloughs, the Chehalis River. There are the bridges. Across that bridge is Grays Harbor College.*

He got a clear picture suddenly of his mom's face. Decided. Determined. He saw the educational path she pretty much forced him onto. His dad expected him to join him at the mill, but his mom wouldn't think of it.

When he put his foot on the brake at the stoplight at Aberdeen, he took the pause to look around. *That's new,* he thought, and read aloud the sign on the right: "Kurt Cobain Under the Bridge Memorial."

Sad, he thought. *Aberdeen's most famous son. A dead rocker. I always think of Cobain as a kid. But if he had lived, he'd be almost as old as I am now. That's weird.*

Doolittle pondered the junction signs above the intersection. 109 north towards Ocean Shores. 105 south towards Westport. He flicked on the left blinker. *The north road ends up at the Quinault Reservation, the south just goes and goes*, he thought. He saw the light turn green, put his foot on the gas and turned left. He said aloud, "Let's do some exploring, Lena."

Chapter 3 – Salt Air

As he sped along Highway 105, Doolittle glanced at the wide view on his right. *I forgot how pretty this stretch of road was*, he thought, *right along the water.* Through the trees, he spotted the low outline of Rennie Island in the bay. *Must be high tide*, he thought, *if you weren't a local, you would totally miss that.*

He remembered that his dad used to call it Stanley Island. *Wonder why somebody renamed it?* he thought. His dad had talked about how on their days off, he and his buddies would motor out to Stanley in their dinghies, to shoot ducks with scatter guns and bring them home for bird-and-beer feasts in one of their backyards.

"But don't ever fish out there," his dad had warned him. "That's where they dumped the sulfur waste from the paper mill." His dad had shaken his head, tossing a cigarette butt into the water, "Plus a whole lot of other unknown stuff. Who knows what other bad crap is submerged around Stanley?"

Sure is a pretty stretch of water, though, Doolittle thought. The road arced slightly to the south, and looking straight ahead, he glimpsed a stretch of blue flat water, all the way to the low green line of North Jetty, at Ocean Shores. He passed a sign on the right for the Chehalis Wildlife Reserve. He remembered when it was just grasslands, back when this stretch of highway was still called Arbor Road.

"That's new," he said out loud, as he passed the sign for Westport Winery Garden Resort. "At least to me."

They made the place look like a lighthouse. Nice, he thought. *But fake.* Those bright red roofs and perfectly white walls. *Looks like a big dollhouse.* He imagined how lighthouses really look. Salt and wind beaten, tired but hanging tough into the sideways rain from the ocean.

At Markham, he drove past cranberry bogs on both sides of the road—the warehouse on the right had a sign that read Ocean Spray—then crossed the bridge over Johns River. How many times had he and his dad motored the dinghy around the bay and up the Johns until it narrowed into a creek, mired in reeds? The memories flipped like black and white snapshots. *I must have been pretty little*, he thought.

He felt a sudden sadness. He recalled that when he was about 12, he had started refusing to go out in the boat with his dad anymore. It seemed so easy back then to just say 'no' to his dad's requests, which got fewer and farther between until they just stopped. Doolittle supposed he was just asserting his own teenaged power, or something, proving he could make a choice. *Dumb*, he thought. *Just dumb and mean.*

The highway turned inland. Cranberry bogs then trees skimmed by in his peripheral vision. Up ahead, he saw the sign for Bottle Beach State Park, another place of sea grass and flat beach that seemed somehow littered with memories of his dad. He had a flash of their dinghy meandering its way through the reeds of Redman Slough. *Wonder if they have renamed that, too?* he thought. *Doesn't sound very politically correct, these days.*

The highway bent south at Ocosta. He remembered his dad mentioning how that area had boomed fast— something about broken promises from the Northern Pacific railroad to make it a hub town--then disappeared almost as quickly, before Doolittle was born. From their slow-putting boat, he remembered only spiky creosoted pilings poking up from oily sheened water, skeletons of wood buildings leaning over or imploded entirely. Like a sad and soggy ghost town. He remembered the remains always gave him a creepy feeling.

Heading south towards Bay City, he could see the water again on his right, flashing pale blue between the thick bushes that lined the road. When his wheels hit the metal of the Beardslee Slough Bridge--the rhythm and thump vibrating up from one great steel I-beam to the next--he felt his shoulders relax. He pushed the down button in the driver door handle, cracking his window a few inches, and inhaled deeply of the salt air. *Westport,* he thought. *Almost to the ocean.*

He looked left at the delta of the Saginaw River, disappearing into the wide, salty Sopun Inlet. Again, all around here lurked early memories of his dad, too many to count and too far back to remember clearly. They were mostly just blurry images, mossy green and sparkling blue, smelling of fish and his dad's cigarette smoke, of damp socks and soggy baloney sandwiches and warm cans of soda from their moldy Coleman cooler.

Doolittle slowed as he approached the T intersection then stopped before the flashing red stoplight hanging above it. The WA-105 sign at the three-way stop gave him two choices: south towards Grayland and Tokeland, north to Westport. He didn't hesitate. After a box truck that read Ocean Gold Seafoods Inc. passed, he signaled and turned right.

He quickly saw the signs on both sides of the highway for Cohassett Beach. The vividly colored photos of vacation homes and condo buildings for rent surprised him. *This was such a sleepy place*, he thought. *I guess progress is inevitable.*

He remembered that his mom had loved Cohasset. She often said it was her 'happy place.'

She had scrimped from her teacher's salary to rent a tiny clapboard cottage on the beach every summer. It was gray, weathered and drafty, separated from the highway noise only by tall grass. But said she loved falling asleep to the rhythmic boom of the waves, waking up to the chilly fog on the beach, listening to the cries of the gulls.

Doolittle pictured her, sitting in her thick chenille bathrobe, her knees up, in the splintery wood Adirondack chair on the tiny porch, holding her mug of coffee with both hands. Her face was peaceful then. His dad would leave them during the weekdays to head back to the mill, and it would just be the two of them.

Doolittle remembered sitting on one of the splintery steps that sagged down to the sand, looking up at her. They didn't seem to talk much. They mostly breathed deep, took long walks along the ever-moving water line, watching the hordes of sandpipers racing the foamy edge on their tiny speedy stick legs.

He loved her face when she bent and picked up an intact sand dollar, then turned to show it to him, before slipping into the side pocket of her big sweater.

He loved how quiet she was here, probably the antidote to nine months of talking in front of a classroom of mill-town kids.

He loved how soft she was here, compared to the sharp-edged shape she presented during the school year, the squared shoulders, the firm jaw line.

He loved her.

He was startled by the sudden sharp memory of Barbara. He had loved her, too. Her softness and her harder parts. He had loved her and somehow--without even meaning to--let her go. The emptiness in his chest felt at once cavernous and small. He had loved two women, and had lost them both.

He passed the big carved wooden 'Westport Welcomes You' sign, then turned right onto Chehalis Avenue. He passed tiny Cohassett Lake on his left, then hit his left turn signal and headed north on Montessano Street. He slowed as he approached the Silver Sands Motel, but the parking lot was full of cars and campers, so he sped back up. He saw the sign for the Holiday Motel, right across the street from the marina, and pulled in. He parked in the 15-minute spot for guests only, got out and stretched his lower back, his hands on his hips.

He patted the blue hood affectionately. "I know you have a shower and a kitchen, Lena," he muttered quietly. "But I'm going to spoil myself a little." He locked the camper, and went in to get himself a room.

Chapter 4 – North Cove

Doolittle spent a couple solitary days in Westport. His motel was around the corner from the Westport Maritime Museum, so he checked that out. He walked the length of Westhaven Drive, along the east waterfront, and ate a crab melt at Bennett's Fish Shack. He sat alone at a table next to the window, staring at the fishing charter boats moving in and out of the small marina.

He took Jetty Haul Road out to Westport Light State Park, found a spot at the far end of the lot, and walked the path out to Point Chehalis. Stood on the sand and watched the waves curl over the rocks of Westport Jetty. He walked the long south loop towards the Grays Harbor Lighthouse, but turned around before he got there.

He found the rows of new three-story buildings behind the big sign that read Westport-by-the-Sea Condominiums depressing. Westport had not changed much since his youth. As a boy, it had been a treat to visit with his mom and dad. Somehow, Westport's magic had disappeared, just as his childhood had.

On the way out of town, he stopped at a small grocery store and bought a couple sacks full of food. He unloaded them into the camper's cupboards and small refrigerator, then headed south on 105.

After what seemed like only a few minutes, he pulled the camper up to the open window in the rangers' booth at the entrance to Grayland Beach State Park.

He handed over his Golden Age Passport—it had come in the mail right before his 62nd birthday—as well as his Washington Driver's License. The Senior Pass gave him fifty percent off the camping fees. He paid the ranger in cash, then drove slowly through the campground. He found the space noted on the neon yellow cardboard slip, put that on his dash as directed, and parked.

He pulled the camper's manual out of the glove box and slipped it out of its plastic cover. He referred to it multiple times, as it was the first time he had set up the electrical and water connections. Doolittle felt a small thrill of accomplishment when he figured both out without breaking anything. *Guess I'm easily pleased*, he thought.

There was no sewer hookup in the camping space, but the ranger said there was a dump station near the entrance that he could use on his way out of the park. He read those instructions in the manual, as well, then slid it back into its sleeve and put it away.

He locked the camper, walked around the front and stared down into the empty metal firepit. Its round black middle still had some ashes and an empty pop can from a prior camper. *I'll need some driftwood*, he thought, and followed the sign pointing towards the beach.

He wandered along the sandy path, the grass hip-high on either side. Bright yellow dandelions poked randomly through the lush green bunches of grass. The tufts lessened in frequency as he walked through the dunes, the sound of the waves increasing. The last dune was pure sand, and as he crested it, the coastline stretched as far as he could see in both directions. *This is more like it*, he thought.

He walked across the beach, and stopped at the water line. He stood with his hands in his pockets, watching the breakers rolling and crashing, washing the long shoreline with smooth scalloped fans of gray green water, edged by foam.

He took a couple deep breaths, feeling the salty moist air fill his lungs all the way down into his belly. *It feels good here*, he thought. *This was a good idea.*

He also realized he was hungry. He wandered back to the camper. Inside, he opened a can of soup and heated it in a pan on the propane stove. He picked a spoon from the drawer, grabbed the warm pan and put it on a hot pad on the table. He settled on one of the benches, lifted a spoonful of soup to his mouth, but stopped in mid-air.

"Driftwood," he said aloud. "I forgot the driftwood."

He shrugged, then slurped up the spoonful. *Later,* he thought, and finished his soup.

As the days and nights passed, Doolittle sat in front of quite a few driftwood fires. He walked the beach north and south. When he used up the groceries in the tiny camper kitchen, he thought about heading back into Westport to replenish his stock of canned soups and saltine crackers and oatmeal packets. But he found that idea a bit depressing. He decided he needed a proper shower, and maybe a full hot breakfast.

So, he stowed what little he had spread around, unplugged from the water and electric hook-ups, and backed out of the camping space. When he pulled over and parked at the dump station at the park's entrance, he slipped the manual out of its plastic sleeve, pulled on a pair of yellow dishwashing gloves as he climbed out, and followed the waste dump procedure for the first time. *Pretty straightforward,* he thought, *and not as stinky as I imagined it would be.*

After he buttoned everything back up, he headed out of the park gate, then eased Lena into the southbound traffic on 105. Per the posted signs, he slowed to 35 miles per hour as he passed through the tiny town of Heather, which amounted to a couple of stoplights and more cranberry bogs. *No motels here,* he thought, and sped back up to 50.

He saw a red neon Vacancy Sign on his right, signaled and pulled off into a gravel driveway. He read out loud: "Ocean View Bed and Breakfast." He looked around at the half a dozen bleached white bungalows, and the central bunkhouse with a wide front porch. *This will do just fine*, he thought.

He pulled into a space next to the entry stairs, moved the gear shift behind the steering wheel to Park, and turned the key to off, killing the engine. He glanced up at the 'Come On In' sign posted above the front door, and said to the windshield, "Don't mind if I do."

The next morning, as he wiped the egg yolk from his plate with the last corner of toast, he nodded slightly with pleasure. The hot shower—in which he could stand up straight and fully extend his arms--had felt great. The deep night's sleep and the bellyful of ham and eggs didn't hurt, either. He downed the last of his coffee, tucked a twenty-dollar bill under the cup, then pushed away from his table in the small bay window.

As he opened the front screen door, he raised a hand over his head, saying "Thank You" over his left shoulder, just loud enough for the owner lady wiping down the bar to hear him. Her hands were busy collecting plates and cups, so she just raised her chin in acknowledgement, her eyes squinting into a brief smile.

Doolittle drove south on 105, the late morning sun dappling the road through the scrubby trees that lined the east side of the highway. He glimpsed a faded sign on the right that read, 'Seashore Conservation Area State Park,' and the smaller sign under it: 'Drivable Beach Access 25 MPH.'

While he didn't like the idea of driving on the beach–those pickup truck drivers never stayed under that speed limit, and made walking on beaches like Ocean Shores like trying to cross a busy freeway–taking a look at the ocean beyond the scruffy dunes appealed to him.

Just past the 'Tokeland-North Cove Chamber of Commerce' sign, he made a right turn onto Warrenton Cannery Road, and followed it all the way to where it ended in a sandy gravel turnaround.

He read aloud the royal blue Washington highway sign posted above the beach access road blockade: "In Case of Earthquake, Go to High Ground or Inland." A menacing white cartoon wave was curling high over a tiny white stick man, scrambling frantically up the white bank. He shook his head, muttering, "That dude doesn't stand a chance."

Doolittle had read the round blue and white Tsunami Evacuation Route signs posted regularly along 105, but this was the first one he had seen where a tiny human was about to get smashed by a giant wave. *I guess some people need it spelled out for them*, he thought.

He locked the camper, and walked out to the water line. He looked north then south, and realized he was all alone. It was only him and innumerable seagulls for a couple of miles, each way. *I could get used to this*, he thought.

He pulled back onto the highway, and continued south.   At the Junction with 105 East—which he remembered looped back up and rejoined Highway 101 at Raymond—he pulled into the Shoalwater Bay Casino gas station. He pulled alongside a fuel pump, walked into the office and laid down a fifty-dollar bill, enough to fill up Lena. When the tank registered as full, he replaced the nozzle then moved the camper to a parking space in front of the Smoke N' Spirits. He went inside and bought himself a bottle of moderately priced red wine from Washington state, as well as a medium-sized R&R whiskey.

As he handed over the cash, he asked the young woman behind the register where he could find a grocery store around here. Her dimples deepened in her round face, and as she pointed back north, her long straight black hair swayed. She suggested he try Chief Lighthouse Charley's. She put the wine bottle in a skinny brown paper bag, then slid it next to the plastic whiskey bottle in a larger sack, and handed it across to him.

Doolittle nodded, "Thanks for the info." As he slipped the sack behind his bucket seat, he spied the North Cove Bar & Grill across the street. *I'll have to give that place a try*, he mentally noted.

He drove north and found the Chief's store easily. It was painted bright yellow with hunter green trim, and looked more like a smoke shop than a market, but he parked and went in anyway. As he surmised, there were the typical stacks of wool blankets, piles of sage sticks, a display of wildly colored blown glass, which upon closer inspection were mostly weed pipes and bongs, and every vape tube known to man. But they did offer a display of various local honeys, and there was a basket of fragrant fry bread on the front counter.

He bought a couple pieces of bread, and a bottle of clover honey, then stowed that greasy paper sack behind the driver's seat, as well.

He merged back onto 105, heading north, looking for an actual grocery store. He raised his eyebrows as he passed his Bed & Breakfast on the left—*Feel like we're going in circles, Lena?* he thought. After a couple more miles, he saw a large sign in all caps: 'THE LITTLE STORE.' It was small, but it didn't appear to exist solely to sell tobacco products, so he parked in the spot nearest the front door and went in.

This is more like it, he thought. From a metal rack near the front door, he picked up a black plastic shopping basket by the handles, then wound slowly up and down the short aisles, filling it with provisions. When he couldn't cram in another item—he had collected enough ingredients for many breakfasts, lunches and dinners--he put the basket on the counter next to the check register. Then he walked back and grabbed one large pack each of toilet paper and paper towels.

He laid them on the counter next to the basket and waited. No one showed up to assist him. He leaned over the counter, craning his neck towards the door that opened into the back of the building.

"Hello?" he called. "Hello?" He waited and still no response. He looked around the countertop for a bell to ring, since the front door buzzer did not seem to have alerted the proprietors to his existence. "Um…hello?!" he called a bit louder.

He was just about to really holler, when a tiny woman bustled through the backroom doorway.

"Hi, hi, oh hello. Sorry about that. Butch and I were eating our lunch." She scurried behind the counter and squinted up at him, "Thanks for your patience, sir." She looked at the full basket and paper goods, and continued, "Did you find everything okay? Anything else I can get for you?"

She was so short, Doolittle looked almost straight down at the wide part in her steely gray hair, her two long braids disappearing below the countertop. Her scalp underneath was brown, as were her wiry arms and hands. He couldn't easily place her ethnicity, though. His first impression was perhaps Pacific Islander, but whether that was accurate, and from which region, he couldn't immediately tell.

"Flora!" A man's deep voice came from the back room.

The woman held up one finger, and her eyes creased into a smile. "One minute, please!" She hustled with a blur back through the door.

He heard the male voice, then Flora's, both muffled, then a commotion of metal chairs on concrete floor. Suddenly, a huge man walked purposefully out of the backroom door, dipping his head to clear the top jamb. What struck Doolittle was that this guy was as big as Flora was small.

The man limped up to him, his hand held out, his broad pink face smiling broadly, his short yellow-white hair spiking in all directions.

"Butch," his voice boomed.

Doolittle shook the man's hand, feeling his own hand engulfed by Butch's massive paw.

"You're new around here. Welcome," Butch said, pumping then holding on to his hand. "What's your name, friend?"

"Doc," he extricated his hand from Butch's grip. He grinned, wiggling his hand slightly, feeling it tingle as the blood flowed back into his fingers.

Flora stood close behind Butch, her hands on her hips. "Butch! You did it again! Stop hurting our customers!" She did not even come up to his shoulder, but by Butch's reaction, Flora was clearly the boss. He put his huge left arm around his little wife, his voice now much quieter and supplicating, "Okay, hon, sorry. You're right as usual."

It was only as he watched the couple enjoy their one-arm hug, with Flora's head tilted onto Butch's chest, that Doolittle noticed Butch's right arm hung limply at his side, his hand a snarl of mangled knuckles. He followed the gnarled hand down the pant leg, and saw that Butch wore thick-soled shoes with wide braces extending up and under both sides of his legs.

Butch caught Doolittle's staring. "Logging accident, Doc."

Doolittle looked up at Butch's face. He felt sheepish, caught gaping like that. He was pretty sure his mouth had been hanging open. "Um, I'm sorry about that."

"Don't be sorry. It was a long time ago."

Flora had moved behind the counter and was efficiently ringing up the groceries, and stowing them in four brown paper sacks on the floor at her feet.

Butch gestured at Flora, "And besides. Turned out to be the best thing that ever happened to me. Flora was my nurse."

Flora looked up briefly from her work, and blew Butch a silent kiss. Doolittle could see by the light in

Butch's eyes as he just as silently caught it on his ruddy cheek that these two had something special.

Butch turned his attention back to Doolittle, "So, you're a doctor. What of?"

"Oh no. Doc is just my nickname. The name's Doolittle. David Doolittle." He put his hands in his front pockets and smiled. "But only my mom ever called me David. My friends just call me Doc."

Butch nodded, "I see. Well, I sure understand that. My full name is Don Lindstrom, of the logging Lindstroms around here. But my old man was also Don Lindstrom, so I guess that's why everybody just called me Butch."

Flora rang up the total on the register, and just pointed at the amount, catching Doolittle's attention. He pulled his wallet from his back pocket and counted out the bills on the countertop in front of her. She stowed the bills, counted out his change in his open palm, then scooted the full bags around the floor with her foot, until he could lean over and lift them.

Butch held up his left hand apologetically, "I'd help you load up your bags, Doc, but I don't do so well with that front door jamb." He motioned towards the door with his left arm.

"No problem, I got it." Doolittle carried two sacks out to the camper, stowing them via the side door, then made two more trips for the extra sacks, then the toilet paper and paper towels. He closed the camper door, then came back in to say thanks and goodbye to Flora and Butch.

He turned to leave, but then turned back. "Oh hey, I have a question for you two."

Butch and Flora both looked at him, their faces open and helpful.

"Do you know of any place around here where I could park my camper overnight? Preferably by the beach?"

Butch and Flora looked at each other. Doolittle thought he read consternation on their faces, and hurried to add, "Oh, no, never mind. It's no big deal. I can just go find another campground."

Butch cut him off, "No, sir, Doc. You don't have to do that. We know just the place."

Doolittle felt relief. These were nice people, and he certainly didn't want to seem like some demanding tourist.

"It's just funny you ask," Butch said. "We just got a call this morning from the son of one of our oldest friends, Mac. Mac went into assisted living last year, and died a couple months later. His cabin out by the water has been laying empty all this time. We figured his son would want to come use it, but he lives in Arizona now, and can't be bothered. He just asked us to find a realtor to help him rent it or sell it."

Doolittle nodded, "Um, okay. That sounds interesting. Can I go take a look at it?"

"Oh sure," Butch motioned to Flora, who somehow knew he wanted a piece of paper and a pen. Butch leaned woodenly against the counter and drew a map with his left hand. "It's easy. Straight down 105, right on Smith Anderson Road, it's the only cabin out there, nothing past it but driftwood and ocean."

Doolittle took the piece of paper from Butch's outstretched hand. "Thanks, thanks a lot. I'll go check it out now, and then come right back, to let you know, okay?"

"No worries," Butch said, and he and Flora traded a quick look, "We'll be here."

Chapter 5 – The Raft

Doolittle had never thought of himself as a spiritual guy. But there was something about the first time he drove up to Mac's cabin that struck him as serendipitous at the least, and maybe like some kind of big cosmic high-five at the most.

The thought *Oh, here it is* did not seem to just pass through his brain. It registered all through his body, in the relaxation of his shoulders, in a deep breathing into his gut, in the feet-planted thought of *I am where I'm supposed to be*.

And the way it all fell together--without any hassle or pushing or worry—occurred to him as odd, but a good sort of odd. Like somebody up there was helping him out.

He had walked the perimeter of the small weathered cabin, found it was surrounded by scrubby trees on two sides, its big picture windows on the west side facing out over spiky piles of driftwood and the ocean beyond.

He had hurried back to Butch and Flora's store to tell them, "Yes, I'd like to rent that cabin."

But when he walked through their door, he never got to say it. Flora somehow already knew, and was holding the keys out to him. He had taken them from her hand, wordlessly.

Butch explained that the power and water had never been turned off, since they had figured Mac's son and his family would come up to use it a couple times a year. So that all Doolittle needed to do was switch the utilities into his name, and pay a few hundred dollars a month rent, and it was his to use for as long as he wanted.

That night, he had hooked the camper up to electrical--using a long extension cord plugged into an exterior outlet at the corner of the house--and to water with a garden hose. He had made a pot of soup in his cozy camper kitchen, and eaten it, listening to the surf pounding the beach. It reminded him of his mom. And again, it felt like home.

The next morning, he used the house key to let himself in the cabin's front door. He had anticipated that it would be an abandoned hovel, moldy from neglect, but instead he discovered that the inside was surprisingly dry. Everything was covered with a thick layer of dust. Mac's old furnishings were worn but solid, spare but efficient.

The main room was square, encompassing a small living room area, open to the kitchen and dinette on the right, with a door to the single bedroom on the left. He could just see the bathroom door at the rear of the bedroom.

A black cast iron freestanding wood stove—attached to a black pipe that vented through the ceiling--stood on splayed iron legs at the corner between the kitchen and living room.

He read the raised letters on its side 'Comstock Castle & Co., 900 sf.' *The whole cabin is maybe 500 square feet at most*, he thought. *This baby will put out more than enough heat.* He pushed the ornate crown cover open on its swivel, revealing the top lid of the stove, which he could lift to add pieces of wood to the fire, and replace to use as a cook top if the power was out.

The two giant picture windows facing west were cloudy with dirt and soot. *All this place needs is a good cleaning*, he thought.

The next time he visited the store, he had said as much to Butch and Flora.

Again, before he finished speaking, Flora was already handing him a torn piece of paper with something scrawled on it.

He read out loud, "Anita Bickler," and saw below the name was a phone number.

"Nice lady," Flora said, glancing up from whatever she was doing behind the front counter, "Cleans vacation homes for folks up and down the peninsula. She'll straighten you out."

"Oh, thanks," Doolittle muttered, staring at the note in his hand. Flora's apparent telepathy about things was verging on spooky.

"Her husband's dead." Flora looked up, "Just sayin'."

Doolittle nodded, "Oh. Okay."

Having learned by now that the best move seemed to just do what Flora said, he had called the number.

The next morning, when he opened the camper door to brisk knocking, he was surprised. Not by the early hour—Flora had said Anita was a "go-getter"—but by the woman herself.

He had imagined that Anita would be a non-descript little widow lady, white-haired, a lumpy woman in a lumpy apron, cleaning houses to subsidize her meager income.

The lady looking up at him was anything but non-descript. The only part of his preconception that was accurate was her white hair.

But this white hair was bright and shiny, in a long ponytail hanging out of the back of her Seattle Mariners baseball cap. The royal blue of the cap was close but not quite as vivid as her cobalt blue, sparkly eyes.

She looked him up and down, and stepped backwards a couple steps, towards her parked white Mini Cooper. "You Doc?" Her voice was more youthful than he expected, both scratchy and sassy.

He also looked her over. He hoped his glasses and the angle above her on the step hid his appraisal. She was wearing faded blue skinny jeans, a neon green sweatshirt that read 'Ocean Shores Jazz Festival,' and white sneakers. He guessed she was a bit younger than him, but not by much. Maybe 60? But an energetic, fast-moving 60. Certainly not what he had expected.

He nodded, "And you must be Anita." He stepped down the camper's steps onto the pine-needle covered gravel. He nodded towards her vehicle, "Nice car."

"Thanks." She took another step backwards, then put her fists on her hips and looked around. "Well, Flora says you are okay." She looked past him at the camper, "You live in that thing?"

He smiled, "Yep. For now. Guess that's why you're here."

She looked over at the cabin and sniffed, "Good old Mac. He was a nice guy, but a bit of a hermit. Is it a mess in there?"

"No, not really. Just mostly dusty, I think." He felt suddenly embarrassed that he hadn't cleaned it up before she arrived. "Um, I don't have any supplies, or a vacuum, even. Flora said you would have all that."

Anita nodded, "Yep, no worries." She held out her hand, her palm flat and open. "Keys, please?"

He pulled the bunch of keys out of his front pocket, then shimmied the house key off the ring. He handed it to her, "Um, I only have the one door key."

She shrugged, "No problem. I don't need my own key. I can leave this under that flowerpot when I am done, okay?"

He nodded, "Oh, sure. That sounds fine." He felt compelled again to offer to help her. "Um, can I carry anything for you?"

She had already opened the back hatch of her car. She stopped and stared at him. In one hand she held a compact vacuum, and her other hand gripped a large plastic carryall loaded with cleaning supplies. "Uh, nope."

"Okay then." He turned and climbed back into the camper. He felt self-conscious and awkward.

She unlocked the front door, and hollered over her left shoulder in his direction, "Oh, and I take cash or check. No credit cards. When I'm done."

He yelled, "Sure thing!" then pulled the camper door shut. He looked around at his tiny space, felt again that he should be doing something for Anita. *Clearly, I would just get in her way*, he thought. He had only known her for a few minutes, but his first impression was that this woman was a force of nature.

He wasn't wrong.

When Anita was through with it, the inside of the cabin looked entirely different. Not just livable, but somehow warm and inviting. He stood in the front door opening, and marveled at the difference.

After he paid her, and her Mini Cooper had made its small U-turn on the gravel in front of the cabin, she had stopped and rolled down her window. She hollered out at him, "Thursdays. Late afternoons. I can give you two hours every week. Sound okay to you?"

He had given her a thumbs up, then waved with the same hand, as she sped away, her spinning tires kicking up some gravel.

And so they had established a routine. He heated two cans of soup instead of one on Thursday afternoons, before she arrived. He would leave it simmering on the stove while he went for his walk during the two hours she cleaned.

That was the time he usually walked the beach every evening, anyway. He would collect driftwood, adding it by the armful to the large pile he had already amassed, against the north wall of the cabin.

When he returned, it would be dusk outside and warmly lit inside, smelling of cleaning solution and soup. Since it was dinnertime by then, Anita got into the habit of staying for a bowl of soup, a couple of slices of bread and butter, and a glass of red wine.

One evening, Anita reached into her big bag and extracted a cribbage board and a pack of cards. She placed it between the salt and pepper shakers and the napkin holder in the center of the table. Doolittle stared at it, then Anita smiled, "You any good?"

The gauntlet was thus thrown. From then on, after dinner they added a quietly fierce cribbage match. And often, one more glass of wine.

He also walked the beach for a couple hours most mornings. As the days got shorter, and the storms came more frequently, he would find all sorts of junk, tangled amid the seaweed along the waterline. He became so accustomed to the usual colors and shapes up and down the coastline, that anything new would catch his eye immediately. *I'm a true beachcomber now*, he thought.

This particular November morning, Doolittle had been eager to get back out onto the beach after the overnight squall. The previous morning, when he'd gone to the store to load up on provisions before the storm hit, Flora and Butch had explained that November storms could be the fiercest of the year. They had sure been right on about this one.

The noise from the pounding surf and whistling wind had shaken the thin walls of the cabin all evening. As the force of the gale increased, he sat in the recliner, near the wood stove, feeling at once safe and warm in his small enclosure, but also vaguely anxious that the roof might be peeled off the house at any moment.

As it neared midnight, he finally heard the wind die down. He wanted to check out any possible wind damage, so he pulled on his parka, grabbed a flashlight, and walked towards the beach. He picked his way through the larger than usual piles of driftwood. The tide had carried in a massive new supply.

He fanned the light ahead of him as he walked, side-stepping the akimbo debris. In one of the arcs of light, he was surprised by a flash of color.

He shined the light towards it, and sure enough, there was a swath of deep orange where it shouldn't be. *I know this beach*, he thought. *What the hell is that?*

He squinted through the damp lenses of his glasses, trying to make out the shape in the beam of light. As he got closer, he saw that it was a blob six or eight feet long, soft-looking, misshapen, like a big balloon that had partially deflated.

"It's a raft," he said out loud. He moved closer and shined the light around its edges, looking for any markings. There were none. He stepped up to it--the toe of his shoe indenting the side--and peered into the raft. He splayed the light along the interior. At the far end, there was a dark shape, like a big wet blanket or a pile of clothes. He bent forward, and saw the dark wet hair and the cold wet skin.

It was a woman.

Doolittle

Chapter 6 – Madeleine

At first, Doolittle was certain she was dead.

Her wet hair was plastered black against her white skin. Her mouth was slightly open, and her eyes were shut. He picked up a piece of driftwood, and smashed it down hard on another one near his foot. The crack was loud, but she didn't move.

He leaned over the side of the raft, shining his flashlight onto her face. He watched a large drop of water slide off a lock of hair on her forehead and land directly on her eyelid. There was no discernable reaction. Her eyes stayed tightly closed.

He couldn't tell if she was breathing or not.

It suddenly occurred to him that he was definitely not breathing. *Take a breath, dummy*, he told himself. *You're no good to anyone if you pass out.* He looked away from her, and consciously inhaled and exhaled a few times.

He looked up and down the pitch-black beach. There was no light or movement other than his own flashlight. *Yelling for help will bring exactly no one*, he thought. He reached for his cell phone in his back pocket, and felt the space where it should have been. He pictured the phone attached to its charger on his kitchen counter. *No help there, either*, he thought. *Looks like it's all on you, Doolittle.*

He kneeled against the side of the raft, his knees sinking into its rubber sides, then slowly descending to the ground as the air displaced. Once he was stable, he leaned forward. Holding the flashlight with his left hand, he reached out and wrapped his right hand around her forearm. Her skin was wet and ice cold. He adjusted his fingers and thumb so he could feel the veins in her wrist.

He felt himself hold his breath. Nothing. No pulse.

He started to pull away, then felt a slight movement. His fingers barely detected a heartbeat, faint and thready.

"Shit," he whispered. "She's alive."

He laid the flashlight down near his left knee, and reached out to her with his other hand. He continued to hold her wrist with his right hand and cupped her icy cheek with his left.

"Miss!" he shouted into her face. "Hello, Miss!" He held her arm firmly, pulling her up and towards him. Her head started to slump, but he held her face up. "Come on now! Wake up! Wake up!"

He felt her face turn slightly against his hand.

"That's it. I got you. I got you. You are going to be okay. But I need you to wake up!"

His eyes were adjusting to the near darkness, lit only by the flashlight's glow from below them. He was able to see that her eyelids were fluttering.

"That's it! Good job!" he yelled, pulling her up straighter by her left arm, and reaching around for her right shoulder, holding her steady.

She opened her eyes. They were sleepy and unfocused.

"It's okay. I got you. You're okay," he said.

Her eyes widened suddenly, and she sat back, pulling away from him. Her wet arms were slippery, and he couldn't hold her. She fell back against the other side of raft.

She looked around, her eyes wide open now. "Who?" she croaked, "Who?" Her voice was thick and guttural, like when someone is awakened from a dream. She looked back at his face, "Who, who are you?!"

She pushed herself upright into a sitting position, wiped her wet hair back from her face with both hands.

"My name is Doc," he said, sitting back on his heels, increasing the space between them. He retrieved the flashlight, and held it out from himself, shining the light back onto his face. He smiled in what he hoped was a reassuring and not creepy way. "I found you. Are you okay?"

She shook her head quickly, as if she were trying to make herself come fully awake. He watched her mentally checking on her status, wiggling her feet, her legs, her arms, her fingers. She put her hands on her stomach, her hips. She looked back into his face.

"Doc," she repeated. "Okay, okay. Doc." She looked around again, clearly trying to situate herself. "Where am I? Where's…" She brushed her wet hair back from her forehead again. "I mean, where is this?"

"You're on the beach in North Cove," he answered. "Looks like your raft got pretty beat up." He shined the flashlight around its inside perimeter. "See?"

She nodded.

"What the hell were you doing out in that storm?" He shined the flashlight at her face. She quickly raised her hand to shelter her eyes from the glare. "Oh, sorry. Sorry." He lowered the beam, to divert the light from her face. It rested on her torso, so he could still see her features in its glow.

He saw her struggling to formulate an answer.

"It was, uh, a date. A first date. Um, yeah, he took me out fishing. But instead of coming in when the storm started, he took us out farther. He said we would be safer. Ride it out."

He stared at her.

"Yeah, but it just got worse. The waves just were too high. We started to take on water, so, um, he inflated the emergency raft, and made me get into it. And then a wave tipped over the boat, and I floated out. But, um," she put her hands over her face, "I am pretty sure he didn't make it."

"Wow. I'm so sorry," he said. "That's terrible."

But Doolittle wasn't sure if it was terrible or not. He had heard a lot of people explain a lot of situations over the years. And either her 'date' was just plain stupid, or this story was. He sniffed and looked at the freezing, dripping wet woman. *It doesn't matter which right now*, he thought.

"Well, you made it in. We gotta get you dry." He reached out to her and she held her hands up. He gripped her wrists, and stood up from his crouching position, pulling her up along with him. Her legs were shaky, but they held. He held onto her as she stepped over and out of the raft. She looked frantically back at it.

"What about the raft?"

"What about it? It's not going anywhere tonight." He pointed towards the ocean, "The tide is out and the storm is over. I'll take care of it later. Let's get you inside first." He pulled her upright, then handed her the flashlight. "I am going to walk in front of you, and you can light our way, okay?"

She nodded. He saw that she was trembling all over and her legs were rubbery.

"Do you need me to support you? he asked.

She shook her head, but then took one step forward and started to fall. He reached out and caught her, then helped her straighten up.

"Okay, then. So, yes in fact, you do," he said. "Here, hold this." He handed her his flashlight, gripped her left shoulder with his left hand, then reached around behind her and slipped his hand under her right arm. He guided her firmly as they slowly walked towards the cabin.

She watched the ground, swinging the flashlight and making the light wildly arc back and forth in front of them. He picked his way carefully around piles of seaweed and driftwood, checking the progress of her feet, making sure not to let her trip.

They reached the front porch, and he leaned her shoulder against the wall next to the door jamb. In the yellow light from the fixture above the door, he saw fully how drenched she was. He reached out his left hand near her, to keep her from falling, then opened the door with his right hand. He held it open for her, and guided her inside.

She stood uncertainly, her dripping hair and clothes quickly making a puddle on the entry tile. He steered her by her right shoulder towards the bedroom door. He hesitated. He didn't want to scare her. He stopped and reached around the door jamb and flicked on the ceiling light, illuminating the room.

He pointed through the door, "The bathroom is right through there. Get yourself a hot shower," he said.

She looked blankly at his face. He guessed she might be in some kind of shock.

"Is there anybody I can call for you?" he asked.

"Um, I don't know." She shook her head, and moved through the bedroom into the bathroom, turning on the light then shutting the door behind her.

He walked to his dresser, opened the second drawer, and pulled out a pair of flannel pajamas, then pulled a pair of thick socks from the top drawer. He laid them on the chair next to the bathroom door.

He put his cheek against the door and said, "There are fresh towels in that cupboard. I put some PJs out here for you. And some socks. I'll be in kitchen. Making you some soup."

He didn't hear a response, but heard the sound of the shower being turned on.

He heated some soup on the stovetop, then retrieved a couple pieces of driftwood from the pile outside the front door, stoking the fire in the wood stove.

He walked around the living room, turning on a couple of lamps. He set a placement, bowl and spoon for her on the dinette table. He pulled a sleeve of soda crackers out of the box, pulled apart the waxy paper to partially open it, and laid it on the table.

He moved to the countertop and looked down at his charging cell phone. *I should probably call 911*, he thought. He glanced at the wall clock and saw that it read

12:47AM. He looked towards the picture windows—the living room lights reflecting back to him like mirrors--imagining the black sea beyond, slackening but still churning after the storm.

The cold calculus of his police training, as well as his years of casework, informed his thoughts. *If this guy is still out there, they'll be looking for a body, not a swimmer*, he thought. *And I'm not even certain that this story is true. I'll call first thing tomorrow.*

He heard her say, "Doc."

He turned and saw her framed in his bedroom doorway. She was wearing his pajamas and his socks. Her dark brown hair was damp and hung in uneven ringlets, and her face and neck were pink from the shower. She looked exhausted, but she was clearly going to survive.

Doolittle felt his full age for maybe the first time in his life. She looked like a little girl in his oversized PJs, the arms and legs too long and bunching up. He half expected her to ask for a teddy bear, or a bedtime story. *I doubt if she's even thirty*, he thought. *She's just a kid.*

"What's your name, anyway?" he asked.

She looked up at him, with a trace of a smile, "Madeleine."

Chapter 7 – The Brother

Doolittle sipped coffee from his mug, then sat back and watched her eat. More than half the sleeve of saltines was already gone, and she picked up her bowl and slurped back the rest of her soup.

She wiped her mouth with the back of her hand, took a sip from her water glass. "Maddy," she said.

"Excuse me?" Doolittle stood up and reached for her soup bowl, to refill it from the remainder in the pan on the stove.

"Maddy, that's what people call me."

"Ah," he muttered, as he carried the nearly full bowl and carefully set it on the placemat in front of her.

She reached for a couple crackers, and dug in.

"How long were you out there?" he asked. "You and your date, I mean?"

She gulped down what was in her mouth, her spoon stopping between the bowl and her mouth. She looked up at him briefly, "Oh, um, all day." She looked back down at her bowl.

"You haven't mentioned his name."

She looked back at him, and he saw her eyes were a pale gray blue. Her dark brows knitted, "Oh. Brian. It was Brian."

He watched her face. She looked momentarily surprised, then he could see her remembering to look sad. *Hmm*, he thought, *interesting*.

"Well, it's late. We will call the authorities first thing in the morning. The police. Then the Coast Guard. Do you remember where the boat capsized? Roughly?"

"Um, no. I really have no idea. My date..." she paused, taking another spoonful.

"Brian," he said.

She nodded, swallowing, "Yes, um, Brian. He said he knew where we were."

"Okay." Doolittle stood up and carried his mug over to the counter, and placed it in the stainless steel sink. He spoke to the wall. "When you're done, you can sleep in my room."

"Oh, no, that's okay..."

"It wasn't a question, young lady. I sleep a lot of nights in the recliner, anyway."

She nodded, "Well, thank you. Thanks."

He wiped his hands on the dish towel, then turned. "Now, I am going to go pull that raft in, before the tide comes back in." He looked up at the wall clock, then back at her. To himself, he said, *That raft is evidence. I don't want it floating away.* Out loud, he said, "There's an extra toothbrush in the medicine cabinet. Use it, and get some sleep, okay?"

She nodded like an obedient child, "Okay."

"Okay then." He walked to the door, pulled on his parka then grabbed the flashlight from the counter. He saw his cell phone on its charger. He thought of grabbing it, then thought again. As he pulled the front door closed behind him, he said, over his left shoulder, "Good night, Madeleine. Uh, Maddy."

He felt the door click shut, and stood still on the concrete porch pad. He realized he felt tired, but alert. He had spent his entire career waiting and watching in the dark. Something was up, and whether he liked it or not, his instincts were kicking in.

He walked heavily on the gravel away from the door, making sure his steps were noisy. When he reached the corner of the house, he stopped, then crouched, shuffling low past the living room picture windows. When he reached the northwest corner of the house, he stood up slowly and looked inside. He knew she couldn't see him through the window, as the interior lights made it a mirror against the black night.

Madeleine was standing against the counter by the front door, punching in a number on his cell phone with her right hand. He watched her pull the phone off the charger, then hold it to her ear. He noted that her face looked focused, intent, not groggy as it had at the table. She turned her back to him then, but her head movements told him she was talking to someone.

He watched as the fingers of her left hand sifted through his pile of mail on the counter. She lifted up one envelope and appeared to read it aloud into the phone. She replaced it and straightened the pile.

After what seemed like about a minute, she ended the call, and turned back towards him. He watched as she pressed different buttons on the phone, then reconnected the phone to its charger, replacing it carefully on the counter. She put her hands on her hips and looked around the living room.

Even though Doolittle knew she couldn't see him through the reflection, he felt himself draw back slightly.

She moved her bowl and glass over to the sink, then stretched. She walked quickly around to the bedroom, went through the door, and closed it.

He exhaled, his shoulders relaxing. *Interesting*, he thought. He turned and shone the flashlight on the path towards the beach, and walked that way.

When he reached the raft, he propped up his flashlight between two large rocks, so that the beam shined at the dark orange mass. He bent and used both hands to grip its damp rubber sides and reef it up and over the piles of seaweed and driftwood upon which it was caught.

"Oof," he grunted, as he pulled the raft over the debris and onto the sandy path. It was big and wet and heavy, and he felt his lower back twinge with the effort. After he laid it out on the sand, he picked up the flashlight and examined it closely.

"Rocks never did this," he said out loud. He held the light closer and squinted at the rows of jagged holes that went through one side of the raft. "Bullets did."

He put down the flashlight again, and rolled the raft from one end to the other, pushing out the air pockets, like a thick awkward sleeping bag.

"Oof," he said again as he lifted the roll under one arm, then bent and reached for the flashlight. He straightened up, shifting the rolled raft on his right hip, and followed his flashlight beam back to the house.

He stowed the raft inside the camper, locked its door, then went into the house. It was quiet. He locked the front door, looked down at his cell phone, selected the green phone icon, then pushed the Recent Calls button. There were none. *She erased the call*, he thought.

He had forgotten to retrieve his toothbrush from the bathroom, so he poured a few ounces of whiskey from the R&R bottle into his mug. He drank it in one gulp, then bent over the running water in the kitchen sink, using his finger to clean his teeth. *Whatever works*, he thought, then walked slowly from one light fixture to the next, turning them off.

He pulled a plaid blanket from the basket on the floor next to the recliner, and settled his body into the chair. He could hear Madeleine's steady breathing through the bedroom door. *She's asleep*, he thought. He glanced at the wall clock, and saw that it was after three. *And so should I be.*

Doolittle awoke with a start. Dim light was coming in the picture windows. It was early. He heard a car door slam outside. Then sharp knocks on the front door. He sat up, struggling to find the lever to put the footrest down. His lower back was stiff, and he floundered like a turtle on its back.

As Madeleine rushed from the bedroom to the front door, she said, "I got it." She unlocked and opened the door, revealing a man in a black sweat suit and baseball cap. "Raymond!" she said too loudly, opening her arms wide. Doolittle saw that she had changed back into her own clothes. They looked damp and sandy.

The man glanced over at Doolittle, then took a large step inside, moving woodenly into her embrace. His hands patted her back briefly, then he stepped back.

She turned towards him, her face brightly cheerful, "Doc, this is Raymond! My brother!"

Doolittle gave up on finding the lever, threw the blanket onto the couch, and swung his right leg over the footrest. He clumsily pushed himself up and away from the chair. He moved towards the door, his right hand held out.

"Raymond," he said.

Madeleine gestured towards him, "And Raymond, this is Doc. The man I told you about."

The man stepped forward and shook Doolittle's hand briskly, then dropped his hands to his sides. "Um, yes sir. I mean, thanks."

Doolittle looked at them both, "Well, don't just stand there, come in, come in." He moved past them into the kitchen. He lifted the glass carafe out of the coffee maker, and filled it with water in the sink. "Can I offer you some coffee?"

Madeleine and Raymond exchanged looks. She said, "Oh, that's okay, Doc. You have done enough already."

Doolittle nodded, and turned back to preparing the coffee. "Oh, okay. That's fine." He poured the grounds into the filter, pressed the start button on the machine, then leaned back against the counter, folding his arms. "So, Raymond. You are here bright and early. Where did you drive from?"

Doolittle opened the refrigerator, pulled out the carton of milk from the door, and closed it again. He put the milk on the table, then folded his arms again, waiting for an answer. "Hmm?"

Raymond looked at Madeleine, then back at him. "Um, from Seattle, sir. The Seattle area."

"I see. Wow. That's a long drive. Two and half hours in the best of traffic."
He looked at Madeleine.

"Oh, Doc, I forgot to tell you," she said. "I borrowed your phone last night to call Raymond. I hope that's okay." She smiled coyly, showing her dimples.

"Did you?" Doolittle pulled a mug from the dish rack and poured in some milk. He held the carton up towards them. "Sure you don't want some coffee?"

They both shook their heads.

"Hmm," Doolittle replaced the carton in the door of the refrigerator, then stood by the machine. The only sound was the dripping of the coffee into the pot.
"Okay then."

She put her hand on Raymond's arm. "We really should be going." She looked back towards Doolittle. "Um, I put the pajamas and socks in the hamper in the bathroom. I can't thank you enough. For everything."

"Oh, I thought we were going to call the police?" Doolittle said. "About Brian? And the boat?"

"Oh, um, Raymond did that last night, didn't you, Raymond?" She looked at his face. He seemed caught off guard, then he nodded slowly.

"Did they find they guy?" Doolittle asked.

Raymond looked at Madeleine, then back at him, "Um, no, sir. No body was recovered as yet."

"That's too bad," Doolittle said, not believing a word. The pot was full, so he poured some coffee into his mug, and stirred it with a spoon from the rack. He held it up and blew steam off the top. "I suppose they'll be calling me? To take my statement?"

Madeleine shook her head, "Oh, um, I doubt that will be necessary, Doc."

Doolittle didn't know how to respond to that. This all sounded way out of the usual procedure when someone was missing after a boating accident. He knew there was a protocol, and this was most certainly not it.

He watched as Madeleine looked at Raymond and silently telegraphed a message. Automatically, Raymond turned towards the door, and she did the same, following him through the open front door.

Doolittle walked over and stopped at the door jamb, holding his coffee. He noted the make, color and license plate of the navy blue sedan. He thought about mentioning the raft in his camper, but then reconsidered.

He held up his mug, "Well, take care then. Goodbye."

Madeleine lifted her hand in a wave as Raymond reversed the car, made a three-point turn, and drove away. The car disappeared past the scrubby brush between the house and the road.

As he shut the door, he said, "Her brother, my ass."

Chapter 8 – A Job

After he had showered and eaten breakfast, Doolittle called Sam at the office. After some pleasantries, he asked Sam to run the license plate. Sam had called him back later that day saying the plate was registered to the GSA. It was a government fleet car.

When Sam asked him what was going on, Doolittle tried to sound nonchalant. "Nothing to worry about here," he said, "I'm retired, remember?"

The days passed, and he fell back into his routine of beachcombing most mornings and evenings, driving in for groceries at Butch and Flora's on Mondays, and getting trounced by Anita at cribbage on Thursday nights.

But in the background, he could feel the low buzz of his instinct. Madeleine's implausible story had switched it on. And it did not seem to want to turn itself back off.

Two weeks later, after his morning walk, when he crested the driftwood pile onto the wide sandy path, he was somehow not surprised to see the navy blue sedan parked in front of the cabin. He saw Madeleine and Raymond, both in dark suits, waiting for him at his front door.

He stepped past them, reaching for the doorknob, "It's not locked. I don't usually lock it." He turned the knob, and pushed the door open. He turned and looked at their faces. "But you knew that, didn't you?"

He gestured for them to come in, and they moved past him into the living room.

"Well, you two clean up nice," Doolittle said.

They settled at different ends of the couch. As Raymond sat, and his jacket opened slightly, Doolittle glimpsed a gun in a holster. He also noticed for the first time that Madeleine held a dark leather folder with a zipper closure.

"Funny," Doolittle said, calmly shutting the door, laying his cell phone on the counter, and attaching it to its charger. "The police never did call me." He moved towards them, then stopped and folded his arms across his chest. "Did they ever find out what happened to Brian?"

"Why don't you sit down, Doc?" Madeleine gestured towards the recliner.

"I think I'll stand." He looked at Raymond, "How's that fleet car driving, Ray? The GSA take good care of its vehicles?"

Raymond's face seemed to flinch slightly, but he was tight-lipped.

Madeleine smiled, then unzipped the folder. "Good one, Doc." She looked up at him, "Or can I call you David?"

Doolittle shifted his shoulders, but stayed where he was, "Sure."

She read from pages in her folder, "David V. Doolittle. AKA Doc. Owner of Doolittle and Choi Private Investigators. Quite successful. Respected, even. Long time married to Barbara Vance, a higher up at the Seattle PD. No children. Divorced. Barbara remarried. Recently retired." She looked at his face, "Did I miss anything?"

"My underwear is black and gray stripes. Hanes." He raised his chin, motioned towards her lap. "Want to add that to your file?"

Raymond shifted in his seat. Madeleine closed the folder on her lap. "No, Doc. We want to hire you for a job."

"I'm retired. You said it yourself." Doolittle planted his feet a bit wider apart, "And who's 'we'?"

Madeleine pulled a badge wallet from inside her jacket, and Raymond hurried to do the same. They flipped them open and held them out towards him almost in unison.

"Treasury Department," she said.

Doolittle leaned closer, scanning both. "Madeleine McCann and Raymond Miller, United States Treasury Agents." He leaned back, put his hands into his front pockets. "McCann and Miller. Sounds like some kind of act."

They flipped the IDs closed and put them back into their coat pockets, again like they had rehearsed the move together. *I rest my case*, Doolittle thought.

Madeleine rested her hands on the folder in her lap. "David…"

"Only my mother called me David," he interrupted her. "For you, Doc is fine."

"Okay, Doc. We know you made a career from surveillance. From my research, there aren't many better out there."

"Again, retired," he said.

"That may be. But we need your help." She looked over at Raymond.

He sat up straighter, and joined the conversation. "Mr. Doolittle…"

Doolittle didn't correct him.

"Mr. Doolittle, sir, we have been running an operation out of Westport. Tracking counterfeiting activities from international waters."

"I thought the Secret Service handled funny money." Doolittle scratched his chin, then put his hand back into his pocket.

Raymond nodded, "You are correct. They do. Before 9/11, the Secret Service worked for us. Under

Treasury.   Afterwards, they got moved to Homeland Security."

"I didn't know that."

"Not many civilians are aware.   And since about 2020, Treasury has been trying to get them back."

"I see."

Madeleine interjected, "Be that as it may, Doc. We are a skeleton crew out of the Seattle office. Activities are heating up, but we can't get any more man-power. And then we found you."

"What happened to Brian?"

"Brian?" Her pallor altered, her cheeks and neck reddening.   She glanced at Raymond, then back at Doolittle. "Brian is dead."

"That much was obvious. But how did he die?"

She sighed. "He was murdered. Shot. We were watching Westport Marina from a boat. Even though the storm was coming up, Brian decided to follow the target boat around the jetty and into open water. Once out there, we had nowhere to hide."

"Yes, go on. How did you get into that raft?"

Her eyes darkened with the memory. "They sprayed us with gun fire. Brian, my partner, was hit in the stomach. Then the boat rammed us. Our boat was cut in half, sinking."

"So, he wasn't your date," Doolittle interrupted.

"No, not my date. When the boat split, Brian and I both dove for it. The waves were crazy high, it was getting dark. Somehow, I found the raft, it must have come loose and self-inflated. I pulled myself into it. I guess it was too dark to see me. The big boat was gone, and I was calling for Brian. But there was no answer."

"You're lucky that raft even floated. One whole side is riddled with bullet holes."

She looked up at Doolittle. Her eyes were moist, but there were no tears. He couldn't tell if she was experiencing real feelings, or acting for his benefit.

"Look," she continued, "we really need your help. We are pretty sure that Brian wasn't the only agent these guys have killed. These are bad guys, Doc. Doing bad things. We are not asking you to engage with them. Just do what you do. Watch."

"Hmm." Doolittle walked to the picture windows, and looked out past the driftwood pile at the line of blue ocean. "Just watch, huh?"

"Yes. We will pay you, of course."

"Hmm." He scratched his chin again. It felt like sandpaper. He needed to shave. "If you've really done your homework, you know I'm not much interested in money."

"No," Madeleine stood up. Raymond followed her lead. She continued, "But we wouldn't ask you to help for free."

Doolittle shook his head slightly, closed his eyes. He pictured Madeleine's cold white corpse-like body the night he found her in the raft. He imagined her partner's bullet-riddled body, sinking forever graveless into the Pacific. *That could have been her,* he thought. He opened his eyes and stared out the window, thinking, *I must be crazy.*

He turned and faced them, resigned. "Alright. What do you need?"

Doolittle

Chapter 9 – Westport

Doolittle pulled the camper into a parking space in front of the small Westport Police Department building. He saw that Madeleine's fleet sedan was not there yet, so he walked around the perimeter of the odd-shaped little building, to get a quick assessment of the size of the unit.

There were three marked squad cars, one unmarked car, one motorcycle with chunky tires, and a hurky-looking pickup truck, with Westport Police emblazoned on its doors.

Those thick tires are probably for beach runs, he guessed.

The number of vehicles behind the tiny building surprised him. On first look, he had surmised it housed perhaps two officers supported by one secretary. This appeared to be a bigger force, unusual for such a small town.

The welcome sign on the highway reported that Westport, Washington had a year-round population of only 2200. The town was comprised of just three main streets: Westhaven Drive on the harbor front, and Nyhus and Harms Streets running parallel behind it.

The cluster of small restaurants and fishing charter storefronts filled the four blocks north of Dock Street. All that remained of Westport proper were blocks of warehouses stretching south--which seemed to be either for boat-building or seafood-processing—and then a few miles of middle to lower-income houses and mobile homes.

The only other major concern in Westport appeared to be the massive U.S. Coast Guard station where Nyhus Street ended, at the bottom of the harbor.   Sitting on a couple of acres, its large governmental buildings and huge vessels moored alongside indicated it was an important installation.

Doolittle rounded the corner of the white shake building as the dark blue sedan pulled into the space behind his camper. Only Madeleine exited the vehicle. *Apparently no 'brother' Raymond today*, he thought.

She met him on the sidewalk, and stood awkwardly for a moment, holding her briefcase with both hands. "Good morning, Doc."

He nodded, "Good morning."

They walked together around the north corner of the building to the entrance. He held open the glass front door for her, and then followed her into the foyer.

As he had imagined, there was a single secretary behind a desk, a plexiglass wall enclosing her cubby to the ceiling.

Madeleine bent and spoke through the small rectangular opening: "Good morning. We have an appointment with Chief Daniels."

The woman gestured towards a clipboard with a pen attached to a string. While Madeleine bent over to sign them in, Doolittle silently read the engraved sign behind the glass: *'Doris Macomber.'*

He aimed his voice at the rectangular opening, "How's your Monday treating you so far, Doris?"

Doris looked up from her desk, her eyes narrowing suspiciously, "Fine, thank you," then looked back down at her paperwork.

"Well, that's just fine," he said, noting the lack of a smile or any other spark of personality. *It's early. Maybe she needs more coffee*, he thought.

Madeleine straightened up. With a small lift of her chin, Doris motioned them towards the row of three chairs against the wall.

Doolittle held out his right arm, "After you," and Madeleine moved past him towards the chairs.

Just as they were bending to sit, Doris said, "Chief Daniels will see you now."

There followed a loud buzz and the steel door next to the front desk opened with a harsh click. Again,

Doolittle stepped ahead and held the door open for Madeleine. She smiled slightly as she passed him. "Chivalry is not dead, it seems."

"No, ma'am," he said, then followed her into the room.

They moved past a quad of conjoined cubicles towards the small glass-doored office at the back of the room. A uniformed officer stood in front of the door, his thumbs tucked in his belt.

Doolittle realized that just as he had with Anita, he had totally mis-imagined the Chief of the Westport Police force. He had pictured an older, heavier, more jaded character, possibly a guy who had taken a post-retirement gig after service in one of the bigger city departments inland.

The man in front of them was maybe forty and extremely fit, the long sleeves of his uniform shirt tight around his biceps. Under thick black hair, his handsome face was deep-tanned. As he held his office door open for them, he smiled briefly, revealing white straight teeth. He was the picture of athletic health, and Doolittle felt a sudden wash-over of insecurities about his own age and condition.

As the door closed behind them, the man held out his hand to Madeleine, "Kimo Daniels." They shook hands, then he reached out to Doolittle. "Welcome."

Doolittle shook his hand, noting the firm grip. Daniels motioned them towards the two chairs in front of his desk. As they sat—Madeleine placing her briefcase on the floor between the chairs--he moved around and sat in his large leather chair.

"So," Daniels folded his arms across his chest, "The U.S. Treasury Department has an ongoing operation here in Westport. In my harbor." He looked at their faces, then focused on Madeleine. "That's something I would have liked to know about, before now."

"Well, sir," Madeleine started.

Daniels interrupted, "You can just call me Chief."

She nodded, "Chief. Yes. Well, Chief, Treasury definitely planned on clueing you in at some point. The Coast Guard is already in the loop."

"Are they now?"

"Well, yes, this is a federal investigation, sir. We like to involve local jurisdictions only after we ascertain the scope of the criminal activity."

"I see."

While Doolittle listened as they volleyed back and forth—a not-so-subtle pissing match between government authorities--he surveyed the office walls. He saw a framed University of Hawaii at Honolulu graduation certificate from about 20 years earlier. A gilded United States Navy honorable discharge dated four years later. And a Police Academy credentials from the following year.

He also noted multiple framed photos depicting surfing in giant curled waves, sunlight glinting through green walls of water and foam, caught from various angles. On the wall behind Daniel's desk was a large framed map of Westport, in the center of the Washington coast.

Notations in different colors of marker pen were neatly lettered at various spots along the shoreline. Doolittle squinted through his glasses and was able to make out 'beach breaks, reef breaks, point breaks, and river-mouth waves.'

He looked back at the photographs, and was now able to recognize that it was Kimo Daniels on his board in most of them, his muscles wet and ripped. He also noted a framed photo on the desk of a large family on a beach. Their intertwined brown arms and broad white smiles echoed versions of Kimo.

Doolittle suddenly realized that it was quiet. He started and looked between Madeleine and Daniels. They were both looking at him, expectantly.

"Oh, I'm sorry." He gestured at the walls, "I was admiring your surfing photos, Chief. Very impressive. Um, did I miss something?"

Daniels squared his shoulders, his stern look softening. *He likes compliments. Good to know,* Doolittle thought.

"I just asked you about your intentions, Mr. Doolittle." Daniels laid his forearms on his desk mat, grabbing a pen with one hand. "Ms. McCann informs me that your specialty was surveillance. But this is a small town. Not Seattle."

Doolittle nodded, opened his mouth to respond, but Daniels cut him off.

Daniels pointed with his left thumb over his shoulder, towards the street, and continued, "That camper I saw you driving will stick out like a sore thumb. Here in Westport, we are strict about boondocking."

"Um, boondocking?" Madeleine asked.

"Unofficial camping on public streets and lands. Strictly prohibited here, and strictly enforced." He folded his arms across his chest again, and Doolittle could swear that he flexed his biceps during the movement. "I won't be able to keep my officers off you in that thing."

Doolittle nodded, hoping to sound humble, "I understand and agree, Chief. When I drove around the marina earlier, before our appointment, I mostly saw pickup trucks belonging to fisherman, guys working on the commercial boats."

Daniels nodded, "Yep. The parking lots are full of those."

"Well, sir," Doolittle continued, "I intend to find myself a beater truck. I can put a couple nets and crab pots in the back. I should fit right in." He shrugged, "If you think that's a good idea, of course."

Daniels nodded again, seeming assured that he was the alpha in the room. "Yeah. Good idea." He smiled, "I might even know about just the kind of truck you can buy. My officer's wife just had another baby. He just said the other day that he needs to sell his pickup and buy a mini-van."

Doolittle found himself disliking this guy. *He wants to be in charge of every detail*, he thought. But he tried to look and sound appreciative. "Yeah. Thanks, Chief. But, um, with all due respect, as you said yourself, this is a small town. Driving a local cop's former rig may not be the best way to fly under the radar."

Daniels pushed back from his desk and stood up, "I would say that's a fair assessment. I was just trying to help. Good luck." He motioned towards the door.

Doolittle and Madeleine both stood, and she bent and lifted her briefcase. Daniels stood firmly behind his desk, and didn't move to open the door for them again.

Seems he has established his turf, Doolittle thought. He moved to the door, opened it for Madeleine, and she walked out into the main room. He looked over his left shoulder as he exited the office, "Thanks for the help, Chief. I'll do my best to be invisible."

"You do that," Daniels said.

Chapter 10 – The Coast Guard

Doolittle and Madeleine walked silently out to their vehicles, and he watched as she got into her sedan. He climbed into his front seat, and waited as she pulled her car in front of his.

He followed her around the few city blocks and through the working marina, then into the gated entrance of U.S. Coast Guard Station, Grays Harbor. He stopped behind her, as she parked at the booth and rolled down her window. He watched as she flipped open her badge wallet, and held it out, her arm extended.

The Coastie manning the guardhouse bent and inspected it closely. They seemed to exchange some words, and the man stood and squinted back at Doolittle. The guardsman waved both vehicles through, walked back into the hut, and said something into a handset as they passed.

Madeleine parked the sedan in a space close to the stairs leading up to the entrance. Doolittle parked the camper in the last space at the end of that row. The camper was too wide and long to fit easily into the space next to her car.

She waited for him to join her, and they walked together towards the double glass doors. He stepped forward and pulled the door open. She smiled as she walked through, "Thanks."

He nodded and followed her across the wide lobby towards the reception desk, the sound of her heels clicking on the vinyl floor. The Coastie who stood up to greet them behind the counter was a young black man, looking trim and competent in his crisply ironed blue uniform.

As Madeleine showed him her ID and spoke to him, Doolittle peered at the name plate above his right shirt pocket. *McAdams*, he read silently. Doolittle also noted the three bars above the guardsman's left shirt pocket. *That young and already decorated*, he thought. *Impressive.*

Doolittle had done his research and knew that while this station covered a more than 3,000-square-mile territory—the 63 miles from the southwestern tip of Washington state on the Long Beach Peninsula to the Queets River Delta about halfway up the coast, and 50 miles into open ocean—what it was mainly known for was search and rescue.

Whether it was rescuing over-confident surfers from the nasty riptides outside Willapa Bay, summer sporties who took their boat show purchases out without a chart or a clue about sand bars and sneaker waves, or crusty salmon fisherman or crabbers who had engine trouble or just hit rough seas, this station was busy, all day and all night.

And while the station's territory might only extend fifty miles west from the coast, the Coast Guard routinely performed rescues in the entire 200-mile zone between land and international waters. Doolittle read that the crews routinely pushed the safety limits of their own marine vessels and helicopters to attempt to bring in those who needed their help.

Respect, Doolittle thought.

He also knew that at least a quarter of this station's busy schedule was focused on law enforcement. And while Doolittle may not have become a policeman, he had trained as one, been married to one, and had worked with them for all of his long career. He felt both kinship and appreciation.

McAdams handed over a guest badge on a lanyard to Madeleine, and then held out another for him. When Doolittle stepped forward and accepted the plastic ID with his left hand, he held out his right hand to the young guardsman.

As they shook hands briefly, Doolittle said, "Thank you for your service, son."

While McAdams' face remained stoic, his eyes crinkled briefly with acknowledgement. He nodded, "Sir."

Madeleine watched the exchange and smiled.

McAdams picked up the receiver from a landline phone, waited for it to connect, then spoke briefly into it. He replaced the receiver, then looked up at them, "The Commander will see you now."

He moved to the end of the front desk and gestured towards a hallway with double doors. After he stepped to the wall and pressed a square, there was a loud mechanical buzz, and both of the metal doors slowly opened towards them.

As they moved through the doors, Doolittle saw McAdams nod smartly at them, then return to his post.

As Doolittle followed Madeleine down the long hallway, he saw over her shoulder that there was a female officer waiting for them outside of an open office at its end. The light spilling through the door illuminated her white hat and blue uniform. She was short of stature, but solid of composure, standing with her feet apart and her hands folded in front, below a column of gold buttons.

He noted that her sleeves had gold stripes at the wrists, and her left pocket was a patchwork of gold medals and various colored ribbons. Her hat also had gold stripes over the blue hat band and a large gold insignia above the blue visor. *Impressive*, he thought, noting her wide shoulders, *I wouldn't want to run into her in a dark alley*.

Madeleine stopped and held out her hand. "Commander. Thank you for making time to see us."

The woman shook Madeleine's hand, and said, "My pleasure." She looked past her at Doolittle, and reached out her hand again. He stepped forward to shake it.

"Ma'am," he said, hesitating as he tried to recall the correct appellation. "Um, Commander."

She smiled as she released his hand. "Commander Cook. At your service, Mr. Doolittle."

She turned and led them into her office. She rounded her large wooden desk and sat down. She was framed by a large window, with ceiling height flags on either side. To her right stood the American and Coast Guard flags, and to her left were the green Washington State flag, as well as a blue one that had a ship, a tree and a whale in the center circle, with 'Grays Harbor County 1855' around its perimeter.

She removed her hat, and laid it on the desktop. Doolittle noted that she had salt and pepper hair, cut short over her ears, and small gold earrings. *Guessing she's about my age*, he thought.

She motioned for them to sit in the two chairs. As they settled, she stretched her hands on either side of the desk pad. "Agent McCann tells me you will be joining our investigation, Mr. Doolittle."

"Doc," he said, as he brushed some invisible lint off his knee.

"Excuse me?" she said.

"Um, Doc. You can call me Doc." He glanced at Madeleine then back at Commander Cook. "If you like, ma'am."

Cook nodded, "Doc is fine." She laid her hands flat on the large desk blotter calendar. "So, um, Doc. Ms. McCann explained that you are a retired investigator, willing to assist us with some surveillance. Is that accurate?"

He nodded, "Yes, ma'am."

"And she advises me that you have been fully vetted by Treasury."

He glanced at Madeleine, then back at the officer, "Um, I suppose so."

"Excellent. We need all the help we can get with this one."

Cook pulled open a low drawer and removed a file, laying it on the blotter. She rotated the file and pushed it towards him. He leaned in and pulled it towards himself.

As he sifted through the papers and black and white photos underneath, she said, "As you can see, our investigation to date has revealed some suspects. Both of those boats," she pointed to two overlapping photos, "appear to be involved. But the operators are never the same. And the ones we have been able to photograph have proven difficult to ID."

He looked up from the file, "Am I allowed to keep this?"

She shook her head, "No. But I can have copies made for you."

He nodded and pushed the file back towards her. "So. Tell me what you know so far. Please."

She leaned back, her desk chair reclining slightly, and clasped her hands below her middle. "We believe there is a large 'mother ship,' if you will. It appears to be of the size and sea-worthiness to stay in the open ocean, outside of our 50-mile purview. Smaller boats – 35 to 40-foot fishing charters -- appear to be bringing shipments into port, and then back out. We believe the incoming freight is counterfeit, and the outgoing is genuine currency. Money-laundering, in effect. The bad for the good."

He nodded. "How much are we talking about here?"

She sat forward, locking eyes with his, "From what we can tell, possibly into the millions of dollars. And that means there are millions of phony bills circulating inland, as well."

"Hmm," he scratched his chin. "So it's big."

She nodded, "Yes. Big and we think international. The fakes are most likely coming out of Canada. That is only about 160 nautical miles north of us, right across the Strait of Juan de Fuca from Neah Bay. Port Renfrew on Vancouver Island is one possible exit point for the counterfeiters, but it could be from anywhere up there, really. It's out of our jurisdiction."

"Are the Canadian Coast Guard assisting you?" he asked.

"Yes and no," Cook said. She cleared her throat and continued, "They have a station at Sooke, on Vancouver Island. It's about 50 or 60 miles west of their main station in Victoria. But their central mission is Search and Rescue. Not law enforcement." She nodded, "And they are kept at least as busy as we are with those activities."

Madeleine finally joined the conversation, "That's why this is tricky, Doc," she said, nodding towards Commander Cook. "As you know, for more than 20 years, the Secret Service has been under Homeland Security, not Treasury."

The Commander nodded, "Just like the Coast Guard. Under that same Act in 2002, we were reassigned from the Department of Transportation to Homeland Security, as well."

Madeleine looked at the Commander, then back at Doolittle. "Yes. And while counterfeit money is bad for the economy--and thus for the country—Homeland Security doesn't classify it as being as crucial as terrorism." She sighed, "So this kind of investigation often falls between the cracks."

"I guess that's why Agent McCann asked for your help," Cook agreed. She stood, her wide shoulders dark against the bright window. Doolittle and Madeleine stood as well.

"Well," he said. "Okay then. Let's see what we can see."

Doolittle

Chapter 11 – Re-Upping

When Doolittle got back to the cabin, he laid on the couch, his arm over his eyes. *Why did I have to find that raft?* he thought. He lay there for a while, watching the light from the picture windows move on the ceiling. Finally, he inhaled and sat up, planting both feet flat on the floor. "Okay then," he said out loud. "Let's do this."

In the bedroom, he kneeled in front of the dresser, and opened the lowest drawer. He pushed both hands under the pile of sweaters, and pulled out a black leather folder with a zip-top. He laid it on the dresser top, then pulled himself up.

"Ooof," he said out loud, wondering if the creak he heard came from the floorboards under the bedroom carpet, or his knees.

He carried the weathered legal-sized document pouch to the kitchen table, and laid it on a placemat. He dragged out a chair and sat down. When he pulled the zipper open, he caught a whiff of the interior leather, and the mildewy smell of old paper.

He was transported to the first time he opened the bag. He and Sam had sat through the Licensed Private Investigator Training together. *Now it's all online,* he mused.

Back then, they had to stuff their butts into too small desks in the airless classroom at Decatur High School out by Dash Point. They had both passed the written tests for their licenses on the first go. They had gone together to the main Washington State Department of Licensing in Olympia and handed in their completion paperwork along with their Police Academy Graduate firearms certificates. They had scraped together enough cash to pay for both of their armed investigator's licenses, plus the one for the office. And they had received their badges and gun permits on the same day.

Ironically, though he was mostly office-bound, Sam had actually used his service pistol a couple of times over the years—aiming it at disgruntled targets of their investigations who had come into the office to settle the score. Once he was even compelled to fire it, hitting a large angry man in the knee, which thankfully caused the giant guy to drop the baseball bat he was swinging at Sam's head.

Doolittle, on the other hand, had never actually fired his weapon at anyone. He liked the size and feel of the .38 Special he bought to carry along with his P.I. Badge. The gun had an old timey look, and it gave him a cool Sam

Spade feeling every night when he holstered up before heading out to work.

But other than at the firing range with Sam, he had never loaded the weapon. He kept the gun in its holster and the bullets in his pants pocket.

Old Andy--the grizzled owner of the Enumclaw gun range—often stood quietly on the sidelines as he and Sam practiced. Andy would grumble that Sam "was lucky to hit the side of a barn," but would remark "that Doc is a natural marksman." Andy described Doc's reflexes as "like lightning," and after reeling in their respective paper bullseyes, said several times that Sam "might as well be blind," but that Doc was a "deadeye."

But Doolittle couldn't care less. He just showed up annually to keep the gun licenses for their office current.

Sam used to kid him that he was 'a lover not a fighter.' But the truth was something deeper.

Early on, it occurred to Doolittle that it was nice to know the gun and bullets were there if he needed them. But he hoped he would only need to fire it if he couldn't find a way to either disappear or to talk himself out of that situation. It's what he thought of as 'fading and faking,' another couple of his superpowers. And luckily, he was so good at both, the need to use his gun had never arisen.

Doolittle looked up from the table. *That was a long time ago*, he thought. He pulled his badge wallet and gun holster out of the pouch, and laid them side by side on the

Doolittle

placemat. He pulled the paperwork out next, and placed it on the tabletop. He let the zipper folder fall to the floor, and smoothed out the papers with one hand. *Expired*, he read silently. *Time to call Sam.*

He punched in Sam's number on his smart phone, then put it up to his ear. As he listened to the ring, ring, ring, he said out loud to the empty kitchen, "How the hell am I going to explain this to Sam?"

He heard Sam's voice: "Doolittle and Choi Private Investigators. How can I help you?"

Doolittle smiled, "It's just 'Choi' now, Sam."

"Doc! Hey, buddy!" Sam's voice carried their history right through the phone. "Uh, yeah, yeah. Old habit. How are you, anyway?"

Doolittle nodded, "Fine. I'm fine. Um..." He hesitated, trying to figure out how to phrase what he had to say.

Sam's voice was quick and sincere, "What is it, Doc? What can I do you for?"

Doolittle exhaled and just said it, "So, how do I re-up my license and gun permit?"

There was silence at Sam's end.

Doolittle pulled the phone away from his ear and looked at the smart phone screen. It showed the seconds clicking forward. The call was still live. He put it back to his ear, and said, "Hello?"

He heard Sam laughing.

"What's so funny?" Doolittle asked.

He heard Sam snort, then chuckle a bit more. Sam said, "Sorry. Sorry, Doc. I just won a bet."

"What? What're you talking about?"

"I bet Lisa that you wouldn't last long doing nothing." Sam chuckled, "And it looks like I just won."

Doolittle sniffed. "Good for you, Sam. What did you win?"

"A home-cooked dinner." Sam was laughing again, but the sound faded. He seemed to have moved away from his phone. He heard Sam say, but at a distance, "Oh boy, she is going to be mad."

"Sam?"

"Hold on. Just a minute," Sam called to the phone. Doolittle heard a filing cabinet drawer slam.

"Here we are," Sam's voice came back to the phone. "You're all good, buddy."

"What does that mean?"

"It means I sent through your renewals on both your badge license and your gun permit a couple of months ago."

"But," Doolittle rubbed his chin. "I retired, man."

"Yeah, yeah. So you keep saying."

He could hear papers rustling, then Sam said, "So, now you're receiving your mail at that Little Store place, right?"

Doolittle nodded, "Yep." He had confirmed that arrangement with Butch and Flora just that morning.

He heard more paper crunching noises, then Sam said, "Well okay, I will make copies then mail you these originals, right after we get off the phone."

Doolittle shrugged, "Don't you even want to know why I need them, Sam?"

Sam said, "You'll tell me when you tell me, Doc. Okay then?"

Doolittle smiled and nodded. "Okay then."

Later, after he had showered, eaten some soup, and washed and dried the pan and bowl, Doolittle drove up to the Little Store.

The door sensor buzzed as he walked through the front door. He was hollering towards the backroom door, "Flora. Butch. It's just Doc," when Flora bustled through the opening.

"Here I am, Doc," she almost sang, running behind the front counter.

He smiled, "Well, hello there."

"We missed you yesterday," she peered at him, her eyes just clearing the countertop. "Where the heck have you been?"

"Well," he started to answer, again hesitating about what and how much he should say to these folks.

Butch's massive form pushed through the back room door, his voice booming ahead of him, "Yeah, that's what I want to know, Doc."

Again, Doolittle marveled that Butch was as big and slow--shuffling his giant braced legs along by holding onto various surfaces—as Flora was tiny and quick.

Doolittle smiled at them both, "I was up in Westport for the day. Just checking it out."

Flora piped up, "Oh, did you eat at the King Tide?" Her hands were busy, sorting and organizing boxes of gum and mints along the front countertop. "Those folks are so nice. And the food is good. Just one entrée per night. Family style."

Doolittle shook his head, "Uh, no, I didn't get the chance…"

Flora continued, "Oh, that lasagna is so good. And one time, they had corned beef and cabbage…"

"Well," he smiled, "I will definitely have to check that out, next time I'm up there, okay?"

Flora nodded cheerfully.

Butch asked, "Anything we can do for you, Doc?" He cocked his head slightly to one side, "You seem like a man on a mission today."

Doolittle paused. *Either I am getting more transparent*, he thought, *or these two are just spooky.* "Well, I'm glad that you ask, Butch, because I was just thinking I should start looking for some kind of pickup truck." He thumbed over his shoulder, towards the front door and the parking lot beyond. "My camper gets pretty bad gas mileage, like seven or eight miles per gallon."

Butch rubbed the stubble on his chin with his good hand, then looked over at Flora. She looked back at him, grinning.

"What?" Doolittle asked. "What is it?"

"It's just funny you ask," Butch said, "We just got a call this morning from one of our oldest friends."

Chapter 12 – Part of the Furniture

Doolittle parked his pickup truck in a space at the far end of the Westport Marina lot, between two other empty pickups. Dusk was settling over the rows of commercial fishing boats on the piers—what this marina called 'floats'--lining the small enclosed bay. He looked up and read aloud: "Float 19."

He was already tired. Getting used to night work was going to be an adjustment, especially after his busy day.

Just that morning, he had handed over a handful of cash to Butch and Flora's buddy, a retired fisherman named Gus, in front of his weather-beaten house in Cosmopolis, across the bridge south of Aberdeen.

Anita had given Doolittle a ride into town. First, he had retrieved the rubber-banded stack of mail from the porch of his folks' old house. Then she dropped him off at

Gus' house on her way to the west Aberdeen Walmart, where she did her weekly shopping.

At Doolittle's request, Gus had wrestled two dilapidated crab pots from the rusting heap leaning against his detached one-car garage, and thrown them into the deal, no charge. Signed title in hand, Doolittle had driven from there to a scrap-yard over in west Aberdeen, and purchased a faded blue rubber trash can as well as a few coils of thick yellow marine rope.

He piled these haphazardly into the bed of the pickup next to the crab pots, then stood back to survey his work. The once-silver truck's paint had weathered to a primer gray, with random chips in the surface, and there were a handful of dents. There was a long low crack in the windshield, and the bed was piled with what looked like old well-used gear.

Yep, he nodded, *this could be a local work rig, for sure.*

As he had driven back towards the ocean, he had pondered how much that route had changed since his childhood. The giant lumber company Weyerhauser had clear-cut the forests all the way down to the water long before he was born, so his memory of the driftwood-lined coast was flatter, a clearer view out around Grays Harbor.

Since then, scrubby trees had grown up along the waterline, their gnarled branches dripping with thick moss. The naturally high water table along the peninsula that fostered the miles of cranberry bogs also lent the trees that swampy bayou look. *This could be Louisiana*, he thought.

And the foothills along the south of the highway had been stubby tree farms –the first in the United States, re-forested by Weyerhauser in the 1940s—which had matured into almost too dense thickets of towering evergreens.

In the darkening parking lot, Doolittle scanned his perimeter. There were only a few lights in the fishing boats moored in front of him. The warehouses behind him were equally quiet, closed for the night. There appeared to be no shift work in these seafood processing plants, unlike the 24/7 boat-building companies closer to the highway.

On the bench seat next to him were his usual supplies: a tall thermos of coffee, another thermos of hot soup, a couple of plastic-wrapped sandwiches he had made back at the cabin, a black baseball cap, an old pair of binoculars, a camera with a long zoom lens, a cassette recorder, and his only nod to modern technology, his smart phone. Its video recording capability was far better than any of his old camcorders. *Time marches on*, he thought, as he unwrapped the first of his two peanut butter and jelly sandwiches and took a bite.

His usual surveillance routine would have been to check out the taverns and restaurants in a radius around his target area, buy some bar food, nurse a glass of beer, play an occasional game of pool, accustom himself to local characters, so he could spot outsiders fast.

Here in Westport, he had counted only about half a dozen small pub eateries on the two main commercial streets flanking the marina. He calculated that it would be far trickier than it was in the Seattle area to fade into the wallpaper in such a small town. *It's a village, really,* he thought, as he poured steaming coffee into the thermos cap and took a sip. *Harder to become part of the furniture.*

He was also used to being able to wander the larger boatyards, such as Shilshole Marina in Ballard, or Fisherman's Terminal on Salmon Bay, between the Magnolia and Queen Anne neighborhoods. Populous, busy, with nameless tourists, wharf and boat workers and vagrants, it was easy to be virtually invisible. *Here*, he thought, *not so much.*

"But," he said out loud, "it should be way easier to spot anything out of the ordinary." His voice sounded lonely in the stale and stuffy truck cab. Gus had obviously been a smoker. Doolittle rolled down the driver's door window a couple of inches, inhaled deeply. The air smelled equal parts of salt water, diesel fuel and crab guts. *I guess that's better,* he thought, and settled back in his seat.

He had long been able to rest with his eyes open, an odd half-sleep where he was aware of both his interior thoughts and any exterior movements. Sam had bragged to customers that "Doc is a human motion-activated sensor," and that was pretty accurate.

For the first few nights, it was mostly quiet. Once, he watched an obviously inebriated guy stumble down the middle of the parking lot, making his way from one of the pubs along the waterfront back to his vehicle. Doolittle saw the man fumble with his keys, let himself into the cab of his jacked up truck, then weave his way out of the lot, heading for the highway.

Doolittle noted that the guy forgot to turn on his headlights, and briefly thought about following him, to make sure he got to wherever he was going without killing himself or others. *It's 2:00 AM and everyone's asleep*, he told himself, *plus not my circus, not my monkeys*.

He imagined that this night would be similarly uneventful. He folded his arms across his chest and was shifting his shoulders back and forth to find a comfortable spot, when he felt his head involuntarily jerk up. *Motion-sensor, for real*, he thought.

Straight ahead of him on Float 17, he saw two figures loading gear onto a charter boat. It looked to be just as Commander Cook had described: a 35 or 40-footer, with tall rigging for long line fishing as well as welded rings along its sides for fishing poles. In the dome of pale blue created by the overhead dock spotlights, Doolittle could just make out the men, one older and bulkier, the other smaller and more spry.

Doolittle figured he was looking at a skipper and a deckhand, just by the way the first one went straight to the cockpit and started fiddling with controls, while the other was doing the bulk of the grunt work, stowing crates and casting off lines.

The engine rumbled to a start, then purred. He noted that the boat's running lights remained off, as the skipper reversed the boat out of its slip and chugged quietly around the float and into the main channel, leaving a silky wake in the inky black water. Only when the boat reached the mouth of the port and headed through into Grays Harbor did its red and green lights blink on.

Doolittle watched the lights move along the channel until they disappeared around the dark mass of the rock jetty. He opened his driver's door and climbed out of his truck. He put his hands on his hips and stretched, grunting deep and long.

"Okay," he said out loud, as he reached in and grabbed his cell phone. Sam had showed him how to swipe from the top of the screen to access the flashlight function, which he did now. *Handy*, he thought as its bright LED light illuminated the asphalt at his feet, *but that old flashlight had a nice heft to it*. He remembered the few times he had been glad to have the 16-inch black metal tube torch as a means of self-defense. *Ah well*, he thought, and scanned the area once more. All was silent.

He pushed through the Float 17 unlocked gate, which opened with a loud metallic creak. He stopped and looked hastily around again, then shuffled carefully down the slippery ramp. It was low tide, and the walkway angled steeply down to the floating dock. He watched his footing as he moved along the slightly tipsy pier to the empty spot from where the boat had departed. He aimed his cell phone light at the short 4x4 post at the corner of the spot.

"Slip #24," he said aloud. "I'll have to check out who rents that."

He stood still and looked around. Nothing moved other than the barely undulating water around him. He punched the app icon on his phone, turning off the light. He stood and let his eyes adjust to the darkness, then followed the pale blue pools of spotlight back up the dock. He stuck his phone in his back pocket, so he could use both hands to hold the cold metal handrails to ascend the steep ramp.

As he climbed back into the cab of his truck, he realized he was breathing harder than he would like. *Somebody needs to exercise more,* he thought, then reached for the other half of his sandwich.

He had settled back into what he thought of as his limbo zone—where his consciousness hovered between total relaxation and complete alertness—when he was jarred by the low thump of a diesel engine. He sat up and saw that his watch said 3:55AM. Out of the pitch black, he saw a pair of green and red running lights round the jetty, move through the port entrance, and motor quietly down the channel. As it passed the first float, the spotlight at its end dimly illuminated the moving boat. *It's the same one*, he thought. *That's weird. It's been gone what, two hours?*

He watched it turn the corner at Float 17, then maneuver slowly into its berth. *Slip 24*, he thought. *It's go time.*

Doolittle felt himself slouch down in his seat. He reached over and pulled on his black cap. He felt himself get slow. Slow breathing, slow moving, slow watching.

He saw figures at the aft end of the boat, then one jumped out. He recognized the deckhand as he leapt easily onto the dock, then scrambled from cleat to cleat, circling them with moorage lines. *That's one*, he thought. *Next the skipper.*

But two other figures climbed out of the boat next. Both seemed as agile as the first guy, and each hefted large dark duffle bags over their shoulders.

That's two and three, Doolittle thought. *Interesting.*

He watched the three figures huddle on the dock, waiting for the skipper to get off board, and then all four scaled the ramp, single file.

Doolittle shifted and reached slowly around into his back pocket to retrieve his cell phone. He touched the sound icon and made sure it was set on silent. He punched the camera icon, then squinted to double-check that the little lightning icon had a line through it signifying that the flash was turned off.

He held the phone just above his dashboard, so the camera in its top left hand corner just cleared the ledge, and clicked it repeatedly as the four men pushed through the Float 17 gate. Only the skipper's face was briefly illuminated in the overhead light; the others were shadowed by their hooded sweatshirts.

Doolittle watched as they split into pairs, the skipper and deckhand walking quickly north towards the businesses; the other two moving swiftly south into the darkness beyond the marina parking lot. He laid his phone carefully on the seat beside him, and exhaled. *Okay then. Two go out, four come in*, he thought. *Interesting.*

Chapter 13 – Just Breathe

"I think I might have something for you," Doolittle said into the air above his kitchen table. He had laid his cell phone on the placemat next to his bowl of soup, and had selected the speaker function. The late afternoon sun was glinting sideways through the picture windows. He had slept all day.

Madeleine's reply sounded tinny, "That's great, Doc. That was way quicker than we hoped."

"Yep," he nodded, "How do you want this stuff? I mean, do you want me to file it when I send you my report every Friday? Or do you want it now?"

There was a pause, and then she answered, "Well, why don't you tell me what you have, and we can go from there."

"Okay then," he said. He detailed his prior evening's surveillance, told her about the charter boat departing with two men and returning with four, described the two large duffle bags, and gave her the float and slip numbers.

"I can text you my photos of the guys. Only the skipper's face is clear, but you might be able to use your fancy facial recognition stuff to get a name. Sam and I never had access to that level of gear."

There was another pause. He could hear scratching and rustling, and assumed she was taking notes. Then she asked, "Were you able to get the name of the boat?"

"Not yet," he said. "I saw it going out and coming back in, but it was all in the dark. I thought I would mosey into town this evening, and check out the boat while there's still some light."

"Okay," she said. "This is great stuff, Doc. Don't risk being seen, if you can help it."

"I can help it," he said. "Besides, my gut tells me these guys only work late at night, when no one is around. And Madeleine?"

"Yes?" she answered.

"Our deal is I help you track down these guys. Get you names and faces. But you do remember that I am retired, right?"

She didn't answer, so he continued, "These last few nights reminded me of a couple things. One is that I am pretty good at this. The other is that I have been there, done that, bought the t-shirt. I don't want to do this anymore. You get me?"

"Of course, Doc," she said. He heard more rustling, like she was shuffling papers. "So, Doc. Did you see what vehicles these men were driving?"

"Not yet," he said. He smiled and thought, *This woman does not like to hear the word 'no.'* He said aloud, "But I will," and pushed the now cool soup bowl towards the center of the table. "And when I do, I will do my best to put those GPS tracker thingies you gave me on the cars. I assume you and your 'brother' Raymond can take it from there, yes?"

There was silence. He still liked to dig her about that dumb lie, and it still seemed to bug her. Which pleased him.

She finally answered, "Yes, of course. Thanks again, Doc."

He nodded, "Okay then," and pressed the red circle with the tiny telephone icon, to end the call.

The sunset was turning the clouds deep orange and pink in the western sky-- the colors muting as they fanned to the east--as he pulled his truck into a parking spot in front of Float 14. He climbed out of the cab, and shrugged his shoulders up and down a couple of times, to loosen up his tight neck muscles. He had forgotten how bad sitting in a vehicle all night made his body feel.

He put on his baseball cap and zipped his dark jacket, then walked north along the waterfront on Westhaven Drive. At the intersection with Dock Street, he looked left and saw the sign for that King Tide restaurant that Flora had told him about.

Seeing the building sparked a memory from when he was a boy. He remembered that his dad had brought him and his mom to a fancy sort of night spot in that same building, sometime in the 1970s. He vaguely recalled the sign had boxing gloves on it, red boxing gloves. He connected the red gloves to the red drink his mother had ordered: 'a Manhattan Up,' she had said. It all felt very grown-up, how he and his parents were eating steak dinners, and his folks were drinking cocktails, and everything.

He crossed Dock Street, then stopped on the corner, snapping his fingers. "Freddie Steele's Ringside Room!" he said out loud. He looked around, embarrassed, but saw that he was alone on the water side of the street.

He smiled, picturing the tall, movie-star handsome owner himself coming to their table, asking his dad, 'Is everything to your liking?' And Doolittle remembered watching the man wave across the restaurant at a lady who had yellow hair and lots of makeup, saying something about 'My lovely wife.' *Was it Harriett? Or Hannah. I can't remember*, he thought.

Doolittle took another few steps, then stopped and snapped his fingers again. "Helen!" he almost yelled. This time, he saw a couple on the other side of the street turn and stare at him. He smiled sheepishly at them, and shrugged his shoulders. *Her name was Helen*, he thought. *The old brain still works occasionally.*

He walked the next block and went into Bennett's Fish Shack. He ordered fish and chips to go, then waited outside until they called his name. He carried the paper sack back along the promenade until he reached his truck. He put the food on the front seat, relocked the driver's door, then meandered back along the water.

He walked down the ramp to Float 16--now barely tilted since the tide was high—and strolled up and down the dock, his hands in his pockets, just a guy looking at boats. He did the same at Float 17, and when he passed Slip Number 24, he barely glanced at the fishing boat. But he noted its name: *Rascal Marie*.

He walked back to his truck, moved the food over to the passenger seat, and drove out of town. He turned right on Jetty Haul Road, drove to the end and parked in the nearly empty lot, admiring the last streaks of color in the western sky.

He sat and ate the two pieces of fried fish, most of the fries and drank a cup of coffee from his thermos. He wished he had brought some kind of hand wipes or paper towels. The napkins that came in the sack were like tiny squares of wax paper, and it felt like every part of exposed skin—his face, his neck, his hands--were smeared with grease. He rubbed his hands hard down his pants legs a few times, leaving oily streaks. *Anita is going to give me a ration of it,* he thought.

He drove back into the marina, and parked a row back from Float 17. The downtown emptied as it got later, and by midnight, he was once again thoroughly alone in the dark. He felt himself enter his long-practiced mental Twilight Zone—neither fully awake or totally asleep—and waited.

He snapped suddenly to attention. His watch read: 2:27AM. He perceived movement both in front and to the side of him. He sat up, slipped on his black cap, and readied the camera on his cell phone.

He watched two men get out of a dark sedan at the south end of the lot, and walk towards the gate atop Float 17. Each was carrying a duffle bag over his shoulder, and from the way their shoulders sagged, the bags were heavy. Doolittle held up his camera and clicked some photos, but he could see that their faces were still shadowed by their dark hooded sweatshirts.

The skipper and his deckhand appeared to already be on the *Rascal Marie.* Though the running lights were off, Doolittle could see smoke puffing from the diesel engine's exhaust pipe. The men descended the walkway to the dock, handed the bags across to the deckhand, and boarded the boat.

Doolittle snapped photos until the boat pulled out of the slip, motored out of the marina, and disappeared into the blackness past the jetty.

He sat in silence, watching the dark sedan at the end of the parking area. History had taught him not to make any quick moves. The darkness worked both ways: it might hide him, but it could also hide others. When he felt confident that there wasn't anyone else in the car, and no one seemed to be around the perimeter of the lot, Doolittle climbed slowly out of his truck.

He patted the gun holster under his left armpit. His jacket was zipped over it, and the bullets were in the right front pocket of his pants, but it was reassuring, nonetheless. He felt for the GPS square he had tucked into his left front pocket. It was there. He locked the driver's door, and walked slowly back to the warehouse wall, then moved south in its shadow towards the sedan. Again, his history reminded him to not walk out in the open, but to get something big and solid to literally have your back, if possible. Plus, instead of having to scan 360 degrees for danger, the building cut that danger zone in half.

When he reached the corner of the building, he peeked around down the street leading away from the marina. It was empty. No cars. No people. He walked to the sedan and stood behind it, using his cell phone to take a photo of the license plate. *Probably stolen*, he thought, *or fake plates. But you never know.*

He noted that it was a newer Mercedes E320 four-door sedan, black. He walked around it, peering into the windows. They were tinted, and even with cupping his hands around his eyes on the glass, he could see only the vague outlines of empty bench seats.

He moved again to the rear of the car. He crouched down, held onto the bumper, and reached into his left pocket. He pulled out the GPS square and pushed the small button on its corner, the red light confirming that it was turned on. He peeled off the self-stick film and reached under the carriage, finding a lip onto which to slide and press it. Once set, he tried to pull it off. It was stuck but good.

He straightened himself, looked around, then walked back to his truck. When he slid into the driver's seat, he realized he had been holding his breath. He forced himself to inhale. *Breathe, dummy*, he told himself. *Just breathe.*

Chapter 14 – Quick Thinking

Doolittle sat up fast on the couch, gasping. He had been asleep all day, and the shadows through the west windows were long and low into the kitchen.

He licked his front teeth, and it felt like fuzz was growing on them. *Ugh. Forgot to brush my teeth*, he thought, as he rose and trudged through the bedroom then into the bathroom, flicking on the light switch.

He gripped the front edge of the bathroom countertop and leaned in close to the mirror, examining his face.

"Damn, Doolittle, you are getting too old for this," he said aloud to his reflection.

He turned on the hot water faucet with his left hand, and bent over the sink, splashing water on his face. He turned off the water, stood up, grabbed the hand towel from its ring, and dried his face roughly. He let the towel drop to the counter next to the sink, raised his chin and closed his eyes, breathing deeply in and out several times. He squeezed a glob of toothpaste onto his fingertip, smeared it on his upper and lower teeth, gulped water directly from the faucet, then spit it out.

He stared again at the mirror. He saw that his eyes were blood red and his chin had a coat of thick gray stubble.

"You look like I feel," he told the mirror, smiling wryly, only one side of his mouth lifting, "Like an old man."

After he had showered and shaved, he felt a bit better. He wrapped the damp towel around his waist, then from the dresser drawers, he pulled out boxer shorts and a pair of socks, jeans and a sweatshirt. He turned and tossed them onto his bed, smiling at the pile of clean clothes.

Anita, you are a God-send, he thought, then sat on the edge of the bed and put his clothes on.

He moved back to the dresser and from its top, mechanically stowed his wallet into his right back pocket, stuffed a handful of bullets in his right front pocket, and slid the second GPS tracker that Madeleine had given to him into his left front pocket. He rubbed the edges of its square shape through the denim.

Just one more chore and I'm done, he told himself as he put his left arm through the holster, then slipped the .38 into it. He walked out to the kitchen to make himself some soup, his socks shuffling on the carpet.

When Doolittle parked his pickup in the space closest to the Float 17 sign, he could see straight down the dock. He noted that the *Rascal Marie* was in its slip. As he exited his vehicle, he looked over its top and scanned the south lot. The black Mercedes was gone.

Madeleine had advised him via text that the owner of the *Rascal Marie* was a local charter skipper named Fred Davis, who hailed from a long line of Westport boat operators, mostly fishermen. She had also shared that Davis owned an older red Ford F-350, and sent along its license plate number.

Doolittle locked his driver's door, zipped his jacket and pulled on his cap. He felt deep-core tired, and realized that he did not have to play act to look like some old guy just moseying around the waterfront.

I couldn't move fast if I wanted to, he thought, as he walked slowly along Westhaven Drive. He saw his own reflection in the plate glass windows as he passed each charter office and seafood restaurant. He looked like he was just lazily window-shopping. But behind his glasses, his eyes were methodically scanning every direction for the red F-350.

He reached the end of the block and stopped at the corner of East Cove Street. He looked up at the three-story lighthouse-shaped structure set out in a grassy area between the street and rock jetty.

Westport Viewing Tower, he silently read the sign, and saw a handful of tourists circling its turret, taking photos from various angles. *Not a bad spot for a wide view of town*, he noted, then continued walking.

He passed a couple of alleyways on his left, then reached the corner of Nyhus Street. He started to turn left, then stopped short. Two cars back from the corner, with its right blinker flashing, was a weathered F-350. He peered at its occupants and recognized them: the skipper Fred Davis was behind the wheel and the deckhand was the passenger.

Doolittle looked quickly down, and covered his forehead and eyes with his right hand. He held this position--looking down but peeking sideways--as the two vehicles in front of the truck made their turns. As the red pickup rolled up to the intersection and stopped, he feigned clumsily tripping over his own feet on the sidewalk, and then stumbled into the gutter, catching himself on the passenger door.

The men inside turned with startled wide eyes, staring at him. He rubbed his hands on the window, then knocked on it. The deckhand first looked at Davis for permission, then rolled down the window a couple of inches.

"What the hell is wrong with you?" he shouted through the gap.

Doolittle grabbed the top chrome strip of the passenger door with his left hand and leaned hard against the window. He wiped his mouth with the back of his right sleeve and smiled stupidly.

"Hey guys!" he grinned. "Would you have a dollar I could borrow?"

The deckhand's face twisted into a grimace of disgust. Davis leaned towards him and shouted out the window gap: "Get the hell offa my truck, man!"

Doolittle wiped his brow with his sleeve, and pouted. "It's just a dollar. Don't you have a dollar? I'll pay you back!"

"Hell you will!" Davis yelled. He nudged the deckhand, indicating the pile of loose change in his open ashtray. "Karl, give this asshole a couple quarters!"

While Karl leaned over and fished out four quarters, Doolittle was pulling the self-stick film off the GPS square from his pocket. Karl pushed the coins with pinched fingers through the gap in the window. Doolittle grabbed at them, but 'accidentally' hit them to the ground. The coins scattered and rolled under the cab.

"Ah, shit!" Davis yelled.

Doolittle bent down then got down on his knees. Cars backed up behind the pickup truck were honking.

"Get the hell out from under there!" Davis bellowed.

Doolittle crouched and reached under the truck pretending to retrieve the coins. He slid the GPS tracker square onto a flat protrusion and pressed it hard. He grabbed two quarters, then sat back, falling hard on his butt against the curb. He held up a coin in each hand, grinning with victory.

"He's out of the way," Karl yelled. "Go!"

The red truck sped around the corner, its tires squealing. Doolittle watched as it turned and saw Karl's upraised middle finger pressed against the window.

Classy, he thought. He rubbed the asphalt and dirt off of his pants legs and sat still. The line of waiting cars passed by him, each with a disgruntled face looking down at him. He gave each one a squinty smile.

When he was alone, he used both hands on the curb to help himself up. He groaned as he straightened, grabbing both sides of his lower back. "I think I broke my kidneys," he said out loud. He saw the other two quarters glinting on the black pavement, and bent over to retrieve them. He looked at the four quarters in his open palm, and shook his head, "No way am I getting paid enough for this."

Chapter 15 – Somebody on the Inside

Doolittle sat on the stump outside the cabin door, his legs stretched out in front of him, his back against the siding. He held his cell phone to his left ear, listening to Madeleine.

He nodded, "Yep, like I said, both GPS trackers are in place. You have all the information that you asked me to get." He sniffed, and rubbed his nose with the back of his right hand. "That should do it then."

He listened some more. *This woman can sure talk*, he thought, and looked out towards the ocean. *It is going to feel awful good to get back to doing nothing.*

"Okay then," he said into the phone. "Yes, yes, you're welcome. Good luck to you. Hope you get the bastards. Goodbye." He pushed the red icon to end the call, then stood and slipped the phone into his right front pocket. It felt good to have the bullets out of there; they were stowed back in the leather pouch with his gun and badge, under the sweaters in the bottom dresser drawer. *Hopefully for good*, he thought. *That's enough of that.*

He tested the front door to make sure it was locked, stowed the key under the flowerpot next to the stump, and walked towards the mounds of driftwood, and the beach beyond.

For the next week, Doolittle had some difficulty adjusting to being awake during the day. He would sit up in the wee hours, drenched with sweat and rushed with adrenalin. He would get out of bed, pour himself a glass of water and sit on the couch, sipping it steadily. Listening to the distant pounding of waves, and feeling the cool air waft through the partially open windows on the south and north walls, he would slowly relax.

He would remind himself that he was safe, he was alone, and that whatever the bad guys were up to, it was not his problem anymore. His eyelids would eventually get heavy, and he would get himself back to bed and sleep hard.

He found that doing next to nothing made the days speed by. His daily routine included his morning walk up or down the beach, eating lunch, reading a book, taking a late afternoon beach walk, eating dinner and going to bed.

On Mondays, he would drive the pickup to the Little Store to grab a few groceries but mostly just to catch up with Butch and Flora. On Thursday afternoons, Anita came to clean the cabin while he was out walking. She would drop off the round pink laundry basket that held a pile of his clean clothes and stow the other matching basket full of his dirty stuff in the back of her car. Then she would stay for dinner and cribbage, almost always defeating him easily.

Doolittle had parked and tarped the camper in a spot against the fir trees to the east of the cabin. He glanced at it often, sometimes feeling a bit wistful about not being more adventurous and taking it out on the open road. But the truth was that this small dependable life felt nice. *Nothing to be ashamed of*, he thought.

It was early when his cell phone rang, vibrating the top of his nightstand. He reached over and grabbed it, squinting at the number. It was Madeleine. He sighed, touched the green circle, then touched the speaker icon. He laid his head back on the pillow, and laid the phone on his chest.

"Madeleine," he said, his voice deep and scratchy.

"Oh," her voice spoke into the air above him, "I woke you up. I'm sorry."

He rubbed his eye lid with a knuckle, "No, uh, that's okay. What's up, kid?"

"Oh, Doc. I don't even know where to start," she said. "Can we meet? Or can I come see you?"

Doolittle grasped both hands above his head, stretching his arms, and emitting a groan. "Um, I'm not awake yet. Give me a second." He placed the phone on the bed next to him and rolled to his left. He got up and went into the bathroom, splashing cold water onto his face.

He came back to the bed, drying his face with a hand towel.

"Doc?" she said, "Are you still there?"

He projected his voice towards the phone, "Yes, I'm here." He dropped the towel on the bed, and picked up the phone. He turned the speaker off, then held the phone to his right ear. "Can you hear me now?"

"Yes," she said.

"Where are you anyway?" he asked.

"Seattle. Back at the office. A lot has happened."

He nodded and cleared his throat. "How about I meet you near Olympia. Do you know the Martin Way Diner? That's about an hour-and-a-half drive for us both."

"Um, sure, yes, that would work," she said. "If it's not too out of the way for you, Doc?"

"No, that'll be fine. I need to go into town for fuel and some other stuff anyway."

"What time?" she asked.

Doolittle picked up his glasses from the nightstand, held the cell phone arms-length and read: "It's 6:45 now. How about we meet there around 10:00?"

"Uh, okay, Doc. I'll be there," she said. "And Doc?"

"Yes?" he took his glasses off with his left hand and rubbed his right eye with a knuckle.

"Thanks."

He nodded, "Okay then," and ended the call.

He stared through the bedroom door, at the morning light coming through the picture windows in the living room. He inhaled and exhaled deeply, then put his glasses back on. He shook his head, and said out loud, "You're a glutton for it."

When he arrived at the diner, Madeleine was already seated in a booth. Her back was against the wall, and she was facing the entry. *Smart,* he thought. *It's what I would do.* She held up her hand as he entered.

He sat down across from her in the booth. He answered the waitress' question, "Coffee, black," then folded his hands in his lap. He looked at Madeleine. "Okay, lady. You got me here. What's up?"

Doolittle was silent as Madeleine talked. She told him that using the GPS devices he had planted for them, she and Raymond along with two Coast Guard personnel had tracked the counterfeiters. Her team had discovered that a credit union located near the mouth of the Hoquiam River was a main money-laundering hub. The duffle bags of fake bills went in. A couple days later, the bags full of real currency went out.

She also said that Doc's identifying of the boat operators as well as the two carriers had helped the team set up a sting. Raymond especially had been certain that they would be able to catch the guys during the trade-off of the bags at the bank. The team was waiting at 3AM to capture the criminals mid-drop, but instead of surprising them, the bagmen had seemed to know exactly where and how many they were.

Doolittle sipped his coffee, then asked, "If they knew you were there, why didn't they just skip the drop?"

Madeleine continued, "No idea, Doc. I keep asking myself that." She sighed and looked at her hands, then back at Doolittle. "The four of us were out in the open, and they were waiting, like snipers. Raymond got behind a dumpster, and was able to cover us, so the two Coasties and I could fall back safely. But he got hit, Doc. He is in the ICU at Swedish Hospital."

Doolittle put down his mug. "Do they think he going to pull through?"

She nodded, "Yes. It looks like he is going to make it."

He exhaled, "That's good."

"But Doc," she said, "There is no way they should have known we were coming. No way."

He nodded slowly. "Who all knew about your operation?"

She counted on her fingers, "Treasury. Coast Guard. Police."

"Why police?" he asked.

She looked at him, "Well, we had to let the local force in Aberdeen know we were coming. So they could stand down and let us deal with the situation. We didn't want any stray players involved."

"Anyone else?" he asked.

"Well, yeah, and the police in Westport, as well. Same reason."

His finger tapped the handle of the mug, "So, theoretically, a whole hell of a lot of people could have known, yes?"

She nodded, "Yes. I guess so."

"Well, guessing got Raymond shot." He scratched his chin, "Somebody on the inside leaked."

As the waitress passed, he held up his mug with his right hand and pointed at it with his left, smiling. She lifted her chin in acknowledgment and returned the smile.

He put the mug down and looked at Madeleine, "We're gonna need more coffee."

Chapter 16 – Regrouping

Doolittle and Madeleine were silent while the waitress poured his coffee. She put the pot down on the end of their table, held her pencil over her notepad, and waited for their food order.

Madeleine ordered wheat toast and a fruit cup. Doolittle asked for the Special, with bacon, crisp, the eggs over medium and sourdough toast. The waitress flashed him a quick smile before she headed to the kitchen.

"Guess she appreciates a man who likes to eat," he said.

"I suppose." Madeleine swirled a spoon slowly in her coffee mug. "You must think we are the Keystone Cops, Doc. What a cluster."

He inhaled and stared at the wall above her head, then exhaled and looked at her face. "No, I don't think that, Madeleine. I do think you are in way over your head."

She returned his gaze.

He continued, "I still don't get why you and your team have been hung out to dry here." He looked down at his coffee, "I mean, it just doesn't make sense. If what you say about the scope of this operation is accurate, Secret Service should be all over this."

She shrugged. "I don't know. I don't get it, either."

"So," he said, placing his mug to the side of his paper placemat, "Let's review so far, okay?" He took a Bic pen from his shirt pocket, clicked the end and began to scribble on the placemat. He drew a circle in the middle then lines out to smaller circles. He pointed to the center with his pen, "So, here is your 'mother ship.' They use multiple boats to transport multiple crews here and here." He drew an arc from the center around to the top of the placemat, "And up north here somewhere is the source of the fake bills."

Madeleine nodded, "Yes, that's what we believe, so far."

"Well," he said, clicking the end of the pen, open and shut, open and shut, "It seems to me that their Westport route is now burnt. And that credit union, too. Whoever tipped them about your op, well, you will have to figure that out later."

He glanced at the pen, made sure the nib was retracted and slipped it back into his pocket. "Right now, it seems to me that you need to know where they are going next. If you even get that chance."

The waitress arrived holding their plates. She put them down adeptly in front of each of them, then put her hands on her hips. "Anything else I can get you right now?' she asked.

Madeleine shook her head. Doolittle gave the waitress a smile, "No thank you, dear." The waitress nodded and walked away.

"Pass the salt, please?" he asked.

Madeleine wrinkled her nose, "Aren't you even going to taste it first? Salt is bad for you, Doc."

He grinned, "I like to live on the edge."

She handed over the salt shaker and he shook it liberally all over his eggs and hashbrowns. Doolittle dug his fork into his egg yolk, mixing it into his potatoes, creating a yellow pile of food. Between quick mouthfuls, he munched on one strip of bacon after another, and slurped his coffee.

Madeleine watched him, scrunching up her nose again. "I'm guessing you mostly eat alone."

He looked up at her, shrugged slightly, then continued eating. She bit gingerly into her toast, and just picked at the fruit cup with her fork.

Doolittle finished his food, then used a corner of toast to wipe up the yellow traces on the plate. He put his fork on the empty plate, wiped his mouth with his paper napkin, then laid that on top.

"Whew," he breathed out. "I was hungry." He smiled at Madeleine, "I haven't had a good old diner breakfast in a while. Used to be my main meal of the day, when I worked nights."

She raised her eyebrows, "Well, I guess that explains it."

He rubbed his eyes behind his glasses, then stifled a yawn, covering his open mouth with the back of his hand. "Wow. Now I'm sleepy. Guess I'm just like Pavlov's dog, except instead of a bell, I respond to bacon and eggs."

She smiled briefly, then frowned. "I don't know who to trust now, Doc."

"Yup," he rubbed his chin, sitting back against the vinyl bench seat. "That's a fair assessment. You don't."

She poked at the uneaten chunks of canned pineapple and peach. "One partner is dead, another in Intensive Care. Treasury says they are sending more agents, but they need to be reassigned from other ops, so no telling when that will be. And," she looked up at him, "I don't know who in our existing team has sold us out. I'm screwed, Doc." She exhaled, her shoulders dropping in unison with her chin.

"Okay," he said, sitting up straight, and pushing his plate slightly forward. *I can't believe I'm saying this*, he thought. "Here's what we should do."

She looked up. "We?"

146

"Unbelievably, yes," he exhaled. "We need to check out the rest of the ports."

She reached over and put her hand on top of his. "Oh, Doc. Thank you."

He looked down at her hand. Her overly grateful tone made him nervous. He withdrew his hand, and dropped it to his side. "Okay," he said. "Ground rules: First, I have boxer shorts that are older than you. We are not 'in this together,' or any other nonsense."

She put her hand in her lap, self-consciously.

"Second," he continued, "I am just a body until you get more bodies, understood? We will make a list of the remaining Western Washington ports and split up and watch them."

She nodded.

"We might get lucky, but probably not. And third, you need to talk to somebody high up your chain of command, and figure out who the hell you can trust. At Coast Guard. At police. You need somebody bigger than you working on that."

"Okay," she said, straightening her shoulders, "Right."

"Because on the off chance that we can somehow retrieve the line on where these guys will operate next, you're going to need some big help to reel them in. Get me?"

"Yes." Her mouth was set, her eyes serious. "Yes, Doc. I got you."

"Okay then." Doolittle extricated himself from the bench seat, straightened up and wiped crumbs from his shirt front and pants. "Looks like we need a map."

Chapter 17 – Back to Basics

Doolittle had to admit that the Google Map on Madeleine's iPhone was handier than the big paper map he had envisioned using.

He stood, holding onto her driver's door, as she sat half-in-half-out of her car, her butt on the seat and her feet on the pavement. He saw her zoom in and out with two fingers, then she held the screen up for him to see.

"The harbor at Ilwaco?" she asked.

He shook his head. "Not practical. They would have to enter and exit through the mouth of the Columbia to reach Ilwaco. Have you ever seen those waves? The Coast Guard is forever rescuing even big boats there. What's next?"

Her fingers moved on the screen. "Hmm," she squinted as she moved the image. "The Port of Willapa?" she asked, "The harbor at Tokeland?" She looked up at him.

"Possible," he said. "More remote than Westport, but it's a possibility." He took out his pen, and wrote Tokeland on a yellow sticky pad. "Next?"

She mumbled as she moved her fingers on the phone, "Ocean Shores? No, that's a Natural Preserve. No harbor there. Hmmm." She looked up at him, "There's really nothing until you get all the way up to LaPush, at Quileute Marina. Everything else is mostly tribal. But that's pretty remote."

"Hmm," Doolittle grunted. "Anywhere else?"

"Then there's only Neah Bay." She held up the phone so he could look at the screen. "Then there's Port Angeles and Sequim and Port Townsend." She pulled the phone back. "What do you think, Doc?"

He puffed his cheeks full of air, then blew it out slowly. "I'm thinking it's not just about the port. It's about proximity to whatever place they are using for the money exchange, yes? The bank or credit union." He pointed at the phone. "Can you look in that thing and see ports and financial spots?"

She nodded, "Sure. Hang on." She used her thumbs to type some text into the search bar, then peered at the tiny bubble icons that popped up. "Here," she said, "Or here." She held out the phone, Doolittle bent over it. She said, "Looks like Tokeland or LaPush."

He wrote those on the notepad, nodding. "Okay then. So, we have our work cut out for us. Tokeland is easy, close. But LaPush is way north. Out of your Coast Guard station's jurisdiction, too. So, let's cross our fingers, and watch Tokeland for a while. Maybe we'll get lucky."

Madeleine nodded and slipped her phone into an inside pocket of her purse. She swung her feet into the vehicle, and put her key in the ignition.

Doolittle released the door, and she closed it. She pressed the button in the door handle to roll down the window, then rested her elbow on the edge. "Do we watch it in shifts or what?"

"No, I got Tokeland," Doolittle said. "You need to talk to that *Rascal Marie* skipper, Davis. Figure out how they approached him, how much they paid him. You know, put some pressure on the guy. They're going to be looking for another carrier boat, right?"

She nodded.

He continued, "And then you need to get back to Seattle and figure out who you can trust at Treasury, who you can tell about the leak. You need somebody to have your back, young lady."

She smiled, her eyes looking tired, "I don't feel so young, Doc."

"Well, compared to me you are." He stepped back from the vehicle.

She started the engine, and looked up at him. "Thanks. We'll talk soon."

He nodded, and hitched his thumbs in his front pockets, "Yes, ma'am. We will."

When Doolittle got back to the cabin, he dropped his car keys and wallet onto the kitchen counter and then went right back outside. He walked straight to the beach, moving quickly on the path between the piles of driftwood. He was angry. At the situation. At the crooked law enforcement systems. At himself.

"Shit," he said aloud at the waves. "Shit!" he yelled.

He looked down at his feet on the wet sand. "Dammit," he said. He looked up and shook his head ruefully. "It's my own damn fault. I just can't seem to say No."

He exhaled and wandered along the waterline. As the foam-edged laps ebbed back, he saw hundreds of sand crab holes exposed, only to disappear again with the next inflow.

That's how I feel, he thought. *It just starts to feel like I can breathe, can relax, and here it comes again.* He dug his toe into one of the open holes, seeing the bubbles coming out of it, the sign that the crab was digging deeper to avoid the invader from above.

The visual stirred up a thought. An idea wound through his head like tracing a pinball through some lame old Pachinko machine. He couldn't quite catch it. But there was something about his foot coming down on top of the hole in the soggy sand.

He looked out at the horizon, the dark blue gray line of sea under the lighter gray distant sky.

He snapped his fingers. "That's it," he said aloud.

He smiled, dug his hands in his front pockets, and walked back towards the cabin.

Doolittle

Chapter 18 – A New Plan

Doolittle looked up sharply when he heard his name called out. The sound seemed to echo across the empty foyer, as did his steps on the vinyl floor as he walked towards the reception desk.

"I'm Doolittle," he told the female guardsman behind the counter.

She nodded, and murmured into the phone receiver she held, "Yes, ma'am." She put the phone down and looked up at him. She motioned with a nod of her head to the double doors to her right, "Commander Cook will see you now."

The young woman stepped out from behind the desk and pressed the square on the wall. The double doors swung towards him, and he waited until they stopped their swing, and stayed open.

Doolittle nodded to her as he walked past, "Thank you." He looked ahead and saw Commander Cook waiting for him outside her office door, just as she had on his first visit with Madeleine.

"No Agent McCann today, Mr. Doolittle?" Cook asked, steering him into her office with her arm.

"No, ma'am," he said. He hesitated behind the two chairs, as she walked around behind her large desk, and sat. Once she was settled, he sat down in one of the chairs.

"Well," she asked, folding her hands under her belt, "What can I do for you today?"

Doolittle cleared his throat. "Ma'am, um, I mean Commander," he scratched his chin, then put both of his hands in his lap, "I think it may be what I can do for you."

Cook sat forward slightly, "Alright. Tell me what you think that is, please."

He inhaled, his shoulders rising briefly, then started. "I believe I know who the leak is in your counterfeiting investigation." He looked past her, through the window and into the sunshine-bright parking lot. *Just say it*, he told himself, *you rehearsed this all night.*

"Go on," she said.

He looked back at her face, inhaled, then continued. "Agent McCann herself appears to be your leak, ma'am."

Cook's eyes widened, but her face was stoic. She seemed to grip her hands more tightly in her lap. "Alright, go on," she said.

"May I stand?" Doolittle asked. He made a sheepish smile, "When I practiced telling you this, I was standing."

Cook looked briefly as if she might smile, but she nodded, "Of course."

Doolittle nudged his chair back and stood up. He pushed it back up close to her desk, and then did the same with the other chair. In the extra space this created, he started to pace slowly.

"She's the only common denominator," he said, looking at the floor as he moved. "I guess I just didn't want to see it, but it's the only thing that adds up. Her first partner is shot on her watch, then a second." He stopped and looked directly at Cook. "She's been calling the shots, see? Controlling this investigation from the start."

Cook nodded, "Yes, Agent McCann has been leading the Treasury team, but this is a serious accusation. Do you have any proof, Mr. Doolittle?"

"Doc," he said, "You can just call me Doc."

She raised her chin slightly in agreement.

He continued, "And no, not really, but that's where you come in. I mean, why I came to you." He put his hands in his front pockets and started pacing again. "It occurred to me that Madeleine kept sending her agents, including me, to the marina to monitor the counterfeiters. But that's like watching one flower waiting for one bee from the hive to show up. Why not just watch the hive itself?"

Cook cleared her throat, and he continued.

"And every time I ask why the Secret Service isn't all over this, she gave me some excuse that they are too busy with Homeland Security and terrorism issues. But then it occurred to me that she is pulling the strings. Does Secret Service even know what she is doing out here? Does Treasury even really know?"

"Hmm," Cook folded her hands on her desktop, watching him.

"I mean, and what the hell am I even doing on this operation?" Doolittle looked up at her, "Excuse my language, ma'am, but seriously. I'm just an old retired P.I., and I suppose it was a bit flattering to be asked to help out, especially after the way I found her in that raft. But this 'damsel in distress' stuff it wearing a bit thin." He stopped and nodded, "Maybe I'm just another way to look like she's doing her best with a small crew, while in fact, she is doing nothing at all. Except protecting the counterfeiters, by controlling this op."

Cook sat up straighter in her chair. "Hmm, these are all interesting points, Mr. Doo..., um, Doc." She hesitated, clearly thinking something over. "It is true that most of the information that I have received during this case has come directly via McCann. Hmm."

Doolittle put his hands in his front pockets and just stood there, watching her, and waiting.

She continued, "I can call a colleague over at Secret Service, confirm what they know—or don't know—about this." She reached across her desk pad and retrieved a pen from its holder, then clicked its end button absently. "And the same goes for Treasury. I can see if their narrative lines up with McCann's."

"Hmm," Doolittle folded his arms across his chest. He was standing with his legs apart, swaying slightly.

Cook looked at him, noting his stance, "I get the feeling you don't think that's quite enough, Doc. Am I reading you correctly?"

He let his arms drop to his sides. "I know I'm nobody," he said. "I guess that's my whole point. If this operation is as big as Madeleine, um, Agent McCann, says it is—pumping millions of fake dollars into our economy, one duffle bag at a time—it seems to me that the full force of the U.S. government would be all over this, trying to stop that flow. Not just one old has-been investigator."

Cook held the pen with both hands, rolling it between her fingers and thumb, "Notwithstanding your humility, Doc, you have a point. So, if the agencies confirm your suspicions, what is it that you think we should do?"

"Go after the hive!" he said, stepping forward. *That came out too loud*, he thought. He calmed his voice a notch, "I mean, you guys have all the cool gear, right? Helicopters. Drones."

Cook nodded, smiling. "Yes, I agree we have some 'cool gear."

"Well," he said, "Instead of chasing the busy bees, as Madeleine would have us do, why not send some of those bad boys out and watch that 'mother ship' you were talking about?"

Cook laid the pen down next to her desk pad. "As I told you already, as far as we can ascertain, that ship has remained outside our 50-mile jurisdiction."

"With all due respect," Doolittle pulled out a chair, and sat in it. "Is that what the Coast Guard has ascertained—or what McCann told you?"

"Hmm," Cook rolled the pen gently with her forefinger.

"I mean," he continued, "Can't you send a drone to check that out for yourselves? Or can that stuff be checked via satellites, or something?" He held out his hands, "I am clearly a novice here. It just seems to me that if you monitor the mother ship, and see what goes back and forth, it doesn't really matter which marina they are sending the fake bills to. You could be waiting for them, wherever that is, yes?"

"I agree," Cook said, pushing back from her desk and standing. "It looks like I have some things to follow up on." She walked around and stood next to his chair, looking down at him. "And what do you intend to do with yourself while all this is happening?"

"I think I should keep doing whatever Madeleine tells me to do, right?"

Cook nodded, folding her hands across her chest.

"I mean, if I'm wrong, I can keep doing my part to help a U.S. Treasury agent catch some bad guys." Doolittle stood up from his chair, and stepped to the side. "And if it turns out that I'm right, you guys get to do your jobs, and I will just keep my old self out of the way."

He stood up and held out his hand. Cook grabbed it, and shook it firmly.

"Okay then," he said, and turned to leave.

"Doc?" Cook's voice stopped him at the door, and he turned back towards her. "Have you ever ridden in a helicopter?"

Doolittle

Chapter 19 – Business as Usual

As Doolittle rounded the tall pile of driftwood on the path from the beach, he spied Anita's car in front of the cabin. He smiled. *I am one spoiled man*, he thought.

As he picked up his pace, he thought what a nice routine they had developed: how nice it was on Thursdays to walk through his door and see and smell his nice clean house, see Anita's smiling nice face, anticipate sharing a nice dinner and a nice game of cribbage with her.

"It's all just so nice," he said aloud as he pushed open the front door.

"What's so nice?" Anita looked up from where she was coiling the cord back onto its hooks on the upright vacuum cleaner.

Doolittle dropped his keys into a small basket on the counter next to the door, dug his cell phone out of his back pocket and attached it to its charger, pulled his wallet from his other back pocket and laid it between the keys and the phone.

He leaned his lower back against the counter edge, and held out both hands, palms up. "All this," he answered. "All that you do here. Every week. It's nice."

She smiled, "Well, I should certainly hope so." She dragged the vacuum across to the small linen closet, and stowed it inside. She shut the door, then turned to face him. "And I brought us a surprise tonight, Doc."

"Oh, what's that?" he asked.

She bent over her large brightly colored carryall, separated the wicker handles and pulled out a bottle. "Wine to go with our dinner," she held it out with both hands for him to see.

"Oh, shoot, I can't," Doolittle said quickly.

Anita's smile vanished. She held the bottle with her right hand, letting it hang at her side.

He hurried to explain, "I mean, I can't tonight. Um, I have plans tonight."

She cocked her head to the left, her eyes squinting at him, "Plans. You have plans. Tonight?"

Dang it, he thought. He felt he had been fairly adept at keeping his two worlds separate—the one with his weekday routines which included Anita, Butch and Flora, and the other which swirled around bad guys, bad money and various government entities—"Until now," he said aloud.

"Huh?" Anita leaned over, put the bottle on the coffee table, then righted herself, staring at him. "What did you say?"

"I said 'Until now.'" Doolittle motioned towards the couch then walked over and sat down at the far end.

Anita didn't sit as he indicated she should. She remained standing, and folded her arms in front of her chest. "What does that mean?" she asked.

Doolittle rubbed his eyes behind his glasses, then held his left hand out towards her end of the couch. "You might want to sit down."

She did as requested, but sat rigidly near the edge of the seat cushion. "Okay, what's going on. Since when do you have 'plans' after dinner?"

"Since a few months ago," he said.

After he had finished detailing his double life— starting with the night he found Madeleine in a bullet-riddled raft and ending with his recent meeting with the Commander at the Coast Guard base in Westport—Anita just sat staring at him in silence.

He drummed his fingers on his knees. "Um…" he started to ask if she had any questions for him, but she suddenly doubled over, laughing.

When she could catch her breath, she said, "You're serious, right? I mean, you aren't just pulling my leg?" She sat back fully into the couch cushions, still chuckling, watching his face.

"Um, yeah, I'm totally serious," he said. "Why is that funny?"

She sat up straighter, smiling, "Well, you just think you know someone, you know?"

"I guess," he said.

She shook her head, "I mean, when you said you had plans, I assumed you had a girlfriend I didn't know about." Her smile widened, "I never figured you for being James Bond!"

He looked down at his lap, embarrassed. "I'm hardly that."

"Well," she brushed the top of her thighs with both hands, then pushed forward and stood up. She put her hands on her hips and grinned at him, "If the international man of mystery isn't too busy, maybe he can heat up our soup while I set up the cribbage board?"

"I think I can do that," he said.

She retrieved the wine bottle, bent and slid it back into her bag. "And we'll save this," she looked up him, "For another time."

That night, after he parked his pickup truck in the small paved lot at Tokeland Marina, he realized he was smiling. *International man of mystery*, he thought. *Yeah, right.*

He felt exactly the opposite in importance, sitting here in the dark, looking down at the ell-shaped dock. His research told him that the marina could accommodate 50 boats, but tonight the slips housed maybe 20 workboats. This marina was tiny compared to Westport, which wasn't all that big.

All around him was silent and black. From his parking spot, he looked past the gently bobbing line of boats, across the dark expanse of the mouth of Willapa Bay. The shoreline on the other side was a blacker line, with only a few scattered lights signifying civilization. *What I am is a stooge*, he thought. *Going where Madeleine tells me to go.*

He sighed deeply. He reached for the thermos, unscrewed the cap and poured steaming coffee into it.

"That wine would go down much better than this, right about now," he said out loud.

He sighed again, took a sip, and settled back against the bench cushion. *Just another night of saving the world,* he thought, *for Bond, James Bond.*

Doolittle

Chapter 20 – A Tangled Web

After Doolittle ended the call with Madeleine, he dropped his cell phone on the couch next to him, and stared at it. He shook his head and exhaled. "She knows exactly what she's doing. Nothing's going to happen at Tokeland," he said out loud.

He muttered, "Oh what a tangled web we weave…" *Who said that?* he wondered, *Was that Shakespeare? It sounds like Shakespeare.*

He stood up, put his hands low on his hips and stretched. After two weeks of nights at Tokeland Marina, his lower back felt like it was shot through with rebar, steely and stiff. "Good thing I'm saving the world," he said out loud.

He trudged to the kitchen, and opened a can of soup. As he was spooning it from the can into the pan, he heard his cell phone ring again.

He laid the can and spoon in the sink, wiped his hands on the dish towel, then hurried to the living room, mumbling, "What does she want now?"

He picked up the phone from the couch, but his still wet hands fumbled it. On the fourth ring, he managed to answer, "Hello!" He heard himself sound too loud and a bit rude. *Whatever*, he thought, *it's just Madeleine again*.

"Mr. Doolittle." The voice was curt and authoritative. "Commander Cook here."

"Oh, gosh. Sorry." He held the phone out and looked at the number. It said, 'Restricted: Government.' He put the phone to his ear, "Commander. Yes, hello. Um, I apologize. I was, uh, cooking my dinner."

"My apologies for calling at dinner time," Cook said. "If now is not a good time…"

Doolittle cut her off, "Uh, no, no. Now is fine."

"I see," she said. "Well, I just thought you should know that you were one hundred percent correct."

"Oh. Wow. Okay." Doolittle sat down hard on the couch. He exhaled, the feeling of deep relief flooding his chest. "Um, okay. That's good, I guess, right?"

"Yes, indeed right," Cook said. "I wanted to make sure to say thank you."

He nodded, smiling. "Well, you're welcome."

"And," she continued, "I was just wondering if you feel up for that helicopter ride?"

"Oh," he said. "Yes, sure, I guess. When would that happen?"

"Tonight," she said. "It's happening tonight. Can you get to Westport ASAP?"

"Um," he stood up, "Um, yes. I mean, yes. But um, ma'am, I mean Commander. Is this what I think it is?"

"Yes, Doc, it is," she said. "Of anybody, I figure you have most certainly earned a seat on that copter. We will have protective gear for you. But you may want to bring your own weapon, just in case."

"Wow. Okay, I mean, yes ma'am. I'm on my way."

He heard her say "Fine," and then the line disconnected.

He stood in place for a few moments, getting his bearings.

He realized he smelled something burning. He looked around the room. "Oh!" he yelled, and ran to the kitchen. He pulled the smoking pan off the burner. Its inside was caked black with what was left of the soup. As he put the pan under the faucet and filled it with cold water, he said, "Guess I'll just have to eat on the way."

By the time Doolittle was turning right onto West Ocean Avenue, the sleeve of saltines on the seat next to him was empty. The front of his plaid shirt was covered with cracker crumbs. He made a left at Montessano Street and then a right at Wilson Avenue, which led straight to the Coast Guard base.

He stopped at the booth, and handed his driver's license and badge wallet out the window to the attending guardsman. While the young man took his two IDs into the hut, and had a brief conversation on the phone,

Doolittle hurriedly brushed the cracker crumbs off his shirt and onto the floor at his feet. The guardsman walked formally back out, handed him his two IDs, and waved him through.

Doolittle parked his truck in a spot near the entrance and saw that Commander Cook was waiting for him at the bottom of the steps. With her blunt cut hair, her wide shoulders and her black combat gear, she looked formidable. He thought for the second time that he would not want to tangle with this woman.

He locked the truck as he got out, and slipped the keys into his left front pocket. Then he felt himself ritually patting his holstered gun under his left armpit, and the bullets in his right front pocket.

Commander Cook walked down and waited near the front of his truck. She held out an armful of black gear. "Here, put this on," she said.

He took the bundle from her. She motioned for him to follow her, and he did. When they rounded the east corner of the building, he saw the Coast Guard dock, with two large cutters being fitted up by a bustling crew. To the right of that, he saw a military helicopter on its pad, its blades just starting to spin.

Commander Cook stopped and looked at him, raising her voice to be heard above the sound of the rotors. "Suit up, Mr. Doolittle. I mean, Doc."

He laid the bundle of gear on the asphalt in front of him. He unzipped his jacket, then unfastened his holster and laid it on top of the jacket on the ground. He lifted the thick black bullet-proof vest from the pile, and slid his arms into it, belting it tightly in front. He retrieved the holster and fastened it under his left arm, then he pulled the slick black windbreaker over the top of that, zipping it up. He felt a bit like a shiny stuffed sausage, but he appreciated the extra safety.

"That thing loaded?" Cook asked, shouting now, as the helicopter rotors were at full-speed.

Doolittle shook his head in the negative. He patted his right front pocket.

"It's a toy without its ammo!" Cook shouted. She folded her arms. "Load it, now."

Reluctantly, Doolittle unzipped the jacket, pulled his gun from its holster, then loaded six bullets into its chambers, snapping it shut. He re-holstered the weapon, then zipped up the jacket. He bent and grabbed the jacket he had been wearing off the ground, carrying it along with him.

Cook nodded curtly, then motioned for him to follow her. When they reached the edge of the helipad, Cook crouched down her head, and signaled for Doolittle to do the same. Hunched over, they approached the helicopter, climbing into it in single file.

One of the two guardsmen in the cabin handed Doolittle a set of large black headphones, attached to a long cord. Doolittle sat in the bucket seat to which he directed, and slipped on the thick padded headphones. They completely muffled any outside sound; he could hear only the radio chatter of the helicopter's crew and the static in between their transmissions.

Commander Cook settled into the seat across from him, put on her headphones, and pulled the microphone wand down in front of her mouth. She leaned towards him, cupping her hand over the mouthpiece.

"Pull your mouthpiece down," she said, her voice crackling through the receivers over his ears.

He nodded, and felt along the band, locating the flexible arm and pulling it down. He mimicked the Commander, cupped his hand over it, and said to her, "Like this?"

She gave him a thumbs up, then leaned forward again. "You don't get airsick, do you, Doc?" she asked.

He shrugged, and pushed his glasses up the bridge of his nose, "Guess we're about to find out!"

Chapter 21 – Doing their Job

The helicopter lifted off the ground with a jolt and Doolittle involuntarily grabbed the sides of his seat. He looked up to find Commander Cook smiling at him.

"You'll be fine," she said, "These are combat pilots. They know their stuff."

He nodded and self-consciously relaxed his tight grip. He cupped his right hand over his mouthpiece, and yelled, "Where is Madeleine? I mean, Agent McCann?"

Commander Cook squinted and put one hand up to her right earpiece. She cupped her microphone with the other hand, and looked over at him, "You don't have to shout, Doc. I can hear you just fine. Speak normally, okay?"

He nodded, "Oh, sorry. Um, so, what's the story with McCann?"

She looked briefly out the window to her right. They were above the two cutters now. She watched as they pulled away from the Coast Guard dock. She motioned with her head slightly, "She's down there. On one of our boats."

Doolittle followed her gaze out the side window, and saw the two cutters entering the channel. He looked back at Cook, "So, what's the play?"

Cook spoke behind her cupped hand, "You were right. The Secret Service was unaware of McCann's op here in Westport. They had already frozen this group's activities out of Port Angeles, choked off all their routes from there. Turns out that only McCann seemed to know they had re-upped activities down here."

Doolittle nodded.

Cook continued, "My colleague at the Service confirmed that they have been dealing with a highly organized group out of Canada, most probably funded by the Russian mafia. They have both the technology and the firepower to move this volume of bills across to Alaska, then down the inside passage, ultimately laundering it here for cash, then transporting it back into Russia."

Doolittle asked, "How long has this been going on?"

"Months and months," Cook replied. "My source said they worked on shutting these guys down in Port Angeles for at least a year. Secret Service lost a couple of agents, as well. This case is personal to them."

"Hmm," he said, "How come they didn't catch them?"

"They got close. But their last op went sideways, an agent was killed, and the ship disappeared into international waters. They are hoping that this time, that won't happen again."

"This time?" he said. "So the Secret Service is on this now?"

"As we speak," Cook said, looking back out the window. Doolittle looked as well, and he saw both cutters move around the jetty and out into Grays Harbor. "They have half a dozen agents on each cutter. McCann has not been read in about their presence. The agents are wearing Coast Guard uniforms. So, she still thinks that she and Treasury are in charge."

Doolittle scratched his chin, "So, what changed? Are we following another charter boat out to the mother ship, or something?"

"No." Cook said, "We are going after the mother ship itself. On your lead, we sent out two drones with magnetic satellite GPS trackers. We dropped a dozen above that ship. One drone was shot down, but the other made it back to shore. It only took one tracker to stick, and we could watch their every move."

"Wow, cool," he said.

"Looks like they got impatient. Our radar confirmed the ship moved into port last night, almost all the way in to Aberdeen. They anchored there all night, and we assume the couriers used a dinghy to land." She smiled at Doolittle, "Somebody we know burned the last charter they used. Guess they didn't want to take the time to find another one."

"Okay," Doolittle continued to watch the cutters' progress below them. "So, what's the next move?"

"We intend to keep that ship from getting back out to sea, specifically into international waters. Those cutters," she tilted her head towards the window, "are heading to the mouth of the harbor to block it. And we are their air support."

"I see," he said.

"The plan is to board the ship, arrest the crew, confiscate any bills—real or fake—and one of our captains will pilot it back to our own dock for processing."

"Sounds straightforward enough," he said.

"Yes," she agreed, "Except they are heavily armed, and history shows us they have no problem killing federal agents. They won't go down without a fight."

Doolittle nodded.

"This is on you, Doc," Cook said. "You got us looking in the right place. And to stop taking Agent McCann's word for everything. So, thanks."

He looked across at her, and inhaled, his shoulders moving up and down, "Not sure you are still going to want to thank me in a couple of hours. This feels like it could get ugly, fast."

She raised her chin, "That part's not on you, Doc. That's just our job."

She looked back out the window, and he watched as her hands mechanically patting her gun holster, then the black squares holding ammo on her belt. She turned and looked over her left shoulder at the pilot and co-pilot. She switched a knob on her headset with her right hand, and said something to them that Doolittle couldn't hear. They must have responded, because she nodded, turned and resettled in her seat.

She toggled the knob and said to Doolittle, "We got this."

He felt the butterflies in his stomach flap harder, more like bats or birds, heavy and ominous. *I sure hope so*, he thought, and looked back out into the darkness at the lights of the cutters below.

Doolittle

Chapter 22 – Blockade

Doolittle quickly adapted to the thrum of the rotors that vibrated through his seat. It felt almost hypnotic, the way the rhythm of his dad's diesel boat motor inevitably would relax him into a heavy-lidded daydream state every time they went fishing.

I could almost fall asleep, he thought. He looked across at Commander Cook, watched her upright posture and quick movements. She had toggled her headset channel and was clearly communicating crisp, concise orders. He figured that he had disappeared from her active awareness. She had a job to do, and she was obviously doing just that.

He felt the helicopter's forward movement cease, and the different vibration as they hovered in place. Something had changed. He looked out the window and could no longer see the cutters, only the black of the sea, stretching endlessly west. *They must be right under us*, he thought.

As if in confirmation, Cook touched the knob on her headset, looked at him, and said, "We're here."

"How long can we wait?" he asked, "I mean, how long can we hover until we run out of gas?" He hoped his voice didn't crack with the fear he was feeling.

She smiled, "This is a combat unit, Doc. An MH-60T Jayhawk. It has about an 800-mile range. That's a whole lot of fuel." She looked across the cabin, out the east-facing windows, then back at him. "Besides, radar confirms the ship is only a few minutes away, heading straight towards us."

He felt his stomach clutch. He inhaled and again, hoped he appeared calm. "Oh, okay then." He followed her gaze and saw the lights of Aberdeen twinkling around the far curved edge of the black expanse of Grays Harbor.

The two guardsmen who were sitting in the bucket seats flanking the side door had both been silent and motionless for the entire flight—their black uniforms and weapons somehow merging with the interior of the helicopter like so much anonymous equipment--until now.

The ceasing of the helicopter's momentum seemed to trigger their own. Almost in unison, each guardsman sat up straight, their long guns upright between their legs, their black gloved hands moving methodically, clicking in ammunition magazines, adjusting settings, preparing to engage.

Commander Cook likewise had taken her gun from its holster. She ejected its clip, examined it carefully, then reinserted it in her weapon with a hard snap. She pulled back the top slide till it clicked, then holstered the gun. She looked over at the two guardsmen and nodded curtly. Each nodded succinctly in response.

The guardsman with his back against the co-pilot's seat reached over and grabbed the door handle. He slid the heavy metal door slowly open, the second guardsman grabbing the handle and pulling it the rest of the way. Doolittle felt the shuddering thud through the floor when it clicked into place. He also felt a tickle in the base of his belly, as the helicopter dropped quickly straight down. The falling sensation took him immediately back to when he was a boy, playing on the swings, the way gravity tugged at his pelvic floor after he had pumped himself way up high. *But*, he thought, *unlike this, that was fun.*

He looked around him and saw that Commander Cook and the two guardsmen appeared completely unfazed by their sudden altitude change. *Just another day at the office*, he thought, and hoped again that he did not appear as scared as he felt.

Through the wide door opening, he could now see the two Coast Guard cutters. The two 175-foot Coastal Buoy Tenders were positioned stern-to-stern, about a half-mile apart. Doolittle remembered from his research that the mouth of Grays Harbor was about four miles wide, from Point Brown to the north and Point Chehalis at the south.

Only the green and red running lights fore and aft on the two ships revealed their locations from above. The channel markers on either side blinked, as did the lights from both Westport to the south and Ocean Shores to the north. All else was inky blackness.

Doolittle realized that he was holding his breath. He self-consciously inhaled deeply, then exhaled slowly. *Guess this is what a fish out of water feels like*, he thought. He understood deeply that even with his law enforcement background, this situation was way out of his league.

Commander Cook sat straighter, and touched the toggle on her headset. "Go ahead," she said. As she listened silently, she glanced at her two gunners. They both turned and met her gaze. She nodded to them, then said loudly, "The operation is a go. Proceed."

To Doolittle, it seemed like a lot of things then happened, all at the same time. Each of the two guardsmen dropped to one knee, positioning his long-range rifle on his right shoulder, pointing the muzzle eastward. Floodlights from the belly of the helicopter came on with a flash, as did massive halogen beams on the cutters below. Suddenly illuminated was a large dark ship chugging towards them, mid-channel.

In the lights, it was revealed to be an older commercial fishing vessel, at least 100-feet-long. Dark figures of crew members were seen scrambling into the cabin, and the boat slowed, then came to a full stop. Its prow was pointed directly at the space between the two cutters.

Doolittle felt the helicopter descend again, until it was hovering about 50 feet above the fishing boat's port side. The searchlights bathed the cabin with white light, and the figures within it suddenly had faces, peering up at them. Doolittle counted at least six men.

Commander Cook touched the knob on her headset and spoke into it. Her voice boomed down from speakers on the copter's underside.

"This is the United States Coast Guard," her voice echoed down. Doolittle could hear it muffled through his headphones, and he pushed one side off his left ear.

"Cut your engines immediately and heave to for boarding," Cook said. "Lay down any weapons and come to the port rail with your hands in the air."

Doolittle heard her command, but saw that nothing moved below. *They can't possibly think they can get out of this*, he thought. *There's not a chance in hell…*

His thoughts were cut short by the sudden sharp sound of gunfire. He heard the metallic pap pap pap against the side of the copter as it was sprayed with bullets from below.

The shooters flanking the doorway returned fire, aiming at the source of the flashes. The sound of those shots reverberated in the cabin, and Doolittle replaced the headset on his left ear. He also saw flashing of gun shots from the starboard side of the cutters below them, and heard their muffled reports.

He felt as much as heard another volley of bullets hit the fuselage of the copter. One of the guardsmen flinched, and sat back hard. He appeared to have been hit, but Doolittle could not see exactly where.

Commander Cook unbuckled her seatbelt and lunged towards the guardsman. She pulled him away from his chair and onto the floor, dragging him back towards her empty seat. She took his weapon and moved to his post. She went down on one knee, aimed and fired repeatedly down on the fishing boat.

She motioned with her chin briefly over her right shoulder, and yelled into her mouthpiece, "Help him, Doc!" then recommenced firing.

Doolittle fumbled with the buckle of his seatbelt, then finally felt it release. He got down on his knees, and reached over to the wounded guardsman. The guardsman--his mouth a straight line and his eyes shut--was clutching his left thigh with both hands. The inky black pool spreading out under his leg on the metal floor confirmed the bullet's damage.

Okay then, Doolittle thought, and he felt himself shift into automatic. He reached down and grabbed his cloth civilian jacket, and bunched it up like a pillow behind the man's head. Next, he unzipped his thin military windbreaker, twisted it into a tight twirled rope, and wrapped it around the guardsman's thigh, above where he was holding it.

Doolittle tied the ends into as tight a knot as he could, then pulled one side of his headset off his ear, and motioned for the guardsman to do the same. Doolittle leaned over and shouted into the young man's exposed right ear: "What's your name, son?"

"Tomás," the man replied.

"Tomás, are you hit anywhere else?"

Tomás shook his head in the negative, then closed his eyes and rested his head back against the crumpled jacket. In the glow of the floodlights through the door, Doolittle saw that Tomás' face looked both very young and ashen.

"You've lost a lot of blood, Tomás," Doolittle shouted at him, patting him on his right shoulder. "But you're going to be okay. Hang in there, okay?"

Doolittle swiveled and watched as Commander Cook and the other guardsman continued firing through the opening.

"Got one!" the guard shouted towards Cook, then pointed to the right. "There, Commander, second shooter at two o'clock!"

Commander Cook nodded, aimed and fired.

Doolittle felt one sudden sonic wave of heat after another and the cabin throbbed with bright yellow-orange light. He looked outside and saw that there had been two back-to-back explosions below them, and the helicopter rocked back and forth in their wakes.

"Whew, nice one, Commander!" yelled the guardsman. "Looks like you hit a couple fuel cans, or something!"

In the bright orange glow, Doolittle saw that the guardsman was grinning at Cook.

After the explosions, the shooting from the boat had entirely ceased. Cook yelled something into her mouthpiece, and the sounds of gunshots from the cutter also stopped. Doolittle found the sudden stretch of silence jarring.

Cook said into her mouthpiece, her voice emanating loudly from below the copter: "Line up along your port rail with your hands in the air. Right now."

Doolittle saw the white lights from the cutter grow exponentially, as both cutters approached the boat. The entire length of the fishing boat was illuminated now, and in the light, one after another of the crew moved out of the cabin, and lined up along the port rail, their hands held above their heads, palms facing out.

Commander Cook sat back in the seat, but the other guardsman stayed at the ready. She looked over at Doolittle and at Tomás laying back against the chair.

She clicked the button on her headset, and asked, "How's he doing?"

Doolittle nodded, and she gave him a thumbs up. She turned back and surveyed the action below them.

Doolittle watched over her shoulder as the two cutters flanked the boat. He saw lines get thrown over each side, crew members pulling them tight, narrowing the gap until they could fasten the boat snugly between the two ships.

He saw a cluster of guardsmen from one cutter board the boat, moving behind the line of men against its port rail, grabbing their upheld hands and moving them behind their backs. The men were cuffed, and let by the guardsmen to mid-ship, where they were sat down together in a line against the bulkhead.

Another dozen guardsmen boarded from the second cutter. Doolittle watched as the group split up, one half dealt with the on-board fire, and the other methodically swept the ship, their guns pointed in front of them like long black fingers. He noted that Madeleine was at the tail end of the second group. Then she stepped behind a bulkhead and he could no longer see her.

Commander Cook touched the side of her headset, and asked, "Do we have the captain?"

She listened, and shook her head slightly. "Well, keep looking," she said. "I doubt he got off the boat without us seeing him. Check for any missing dinghies."

She relaxed in her seat, and held the rifle vertically between her legs. She looked over at Tomás then smiled at Doolittle, "Turns out they don't call you Doc for nothing."

Chapter 23 – Always a First Time

The Coast Guard dock was bustling with so much activity, Doolittle decided to hang back and just try to stay out of the way. After he climbed shakily out of the helicopter, he stood and watched numbly as the medics laid Tomás on a stretcher and carried him towards the waiting ambulance.

He noticed that the tourniquet he had made from his jacket was still twisted around the young man's leg. It was shiny with blood, and as he wandered away from the action, Doolittle felt a quick chill. He was glad to have put it to good use, but his holster and bulletproof vest didn't provide much warmth. He realized that he must have left his cloth jacket in the copter, as he felt the breeze off the water go right through his thin flannel sleeves.

He found a quiet corner and leaned against the cold corrugated metal wall of a boathouse. He closed his eyes, and just breathed in and out a few times. The sounds of chopper rotors and gunshots and Commander Cook's booming voice seemed to echo in his skull.

"Doc?" he heard his name and opened his eyes. Madeleine was standing in front of him, smiling. "I thought that was you."

He stared at her face, having no idea what to say. He noted her smug confidence as she continued, "That was something, wasn't it? I mean, we did it. We finally caught them."

Doolittle didn't answer. He suddenly felt deep-core tired. He didn't want to see Madeleine. He didn't want to hear her lies. He shook his head, and the only thing he could think to say in response was, "We?"

There was a shift in her eyes, then she forced a smile, "Of course, we."

He saw over her shoulder that Commander Cook-- with two guardsmen close behind her—were approaching them from the dock. He lifted his chin in acknowledgment, "Commander."

Madeleine turned quickly. He watched her face, saw her affix a professional smile as she outstretched her arm, "Commander Cook, great job. We got them."

Commander Cook stopped about an arm's length from Madeleine, but did not shake her hand. Madeleine put her hand down at her side, awkwardly.

Cook looked past her at Doolittle, "Everything okay over here?"

He nodded, "Yes, ma'am. Just fine." He raised his chin, indicating the long fishing boat bathed with lights at the dock behind them. "You locate the captain yet?"

Cook shook her head, "Not yet. But they are tearing the boat apart now. There are only so many places he can hide."

Doolittle nodded. "I expect so. Do you need me for anything further?"

Cook smiled, "Nope. You go get some rest. That was above and beyond, Doc."

He put his hands in his pockets and moved to walk away. But Cook's next comment to Madeleine changed his mind.

"Agent McCann," Cook said, "May I accompany you to your car? I have a couple last questions for you."

Doolittle could tell that while Commander Cook phrased it like a question, it was clearly an order. He watched Madeleine nod her head in agreement, and then walk towards her dark sedan, parked at the far end of the lot. The Commander walked alongside her, the two guardsmen following about 20 feet behind them.

A loud metallic bang sounded from the cutter dock. He saw both guardsmen stop and turn towards it, their attention diverted.

The next sequence of events would always be a bit fuzzy for Doolittle. They seemed to occur in slow motion, and in no particular order.

Beyond the distracted guardsmen, he saw Madeleine and Commander Cook approach her vehicle on the driver's side. But on the passenger side, Doolittle thought he glimpsed a shadow, which then morphed into a dark figure, and then he could see that it was clearly a man.

Doolittle didn't remember deciding to move towards them, his body just moved. As his walking turned to running, he watched the man lift a gun and point it over the top of the car towards Commander Cook. Madeleine was also looking at Cook, and in the dome of light from above them, he saw that her face was twisted with an odd look of victory.

Doolittle stopped about 20 feet from the car, and found himself transfixed, unable to move. The next thing he heard was a loud gunshot. *Oh my god, they shot Cook,* he thought. But when he looked closer, Cook was crouching low but still on her feet.

Madeleine was lurching in weird slow motion strides towards the passenger side, but Cook straightened and grabbed her arm. Cook simultaneously turned to look back at Doolittle, her eyes large and her mouth in the shape of an O.

That's when Doolittle realized that the man had disappeared. He didn't understand what had happened. Then he felt something in his right hand. He looked down, and saw that he was holding his gun, and that smoke wafted up from the barrel, as if it had just been fired. Next he saw that his holster was empty.

The two guardsmen ran past him then. They split up at the front of the car, one removing Madeleine from Commander Cook's grip, and efficiently handcuffing her. The other guardsman bent and disappeared momentarily behind the vehicle. He stood up, shaking his head. Doolittle heard him tell Cook: "He's gone, ma'am."

Madeleine let out a keening wail, and tried to wrench herself free from the guardsman, but he held her firmly.

Cook walked around the rear of the vehicle, stood for a moment looking at the ground on the passenger side, then reversed and came towards Doolittle. She held out both hands, her voice both gentle and firm. "Okay, Doc. It's okay. You can put that away now."

Doolittle understood that Cook had said something to him, but he honestly had no idea what her words meant. There was a sort of buzzing in his ears, and he just stood there, looking at her face.

Cook reached him, wrapped both of her hands around the gun and took it from him. The second guardsman had followed her from behind the vehicle, and without looking at him, she held the weapon out to one side for him. He took a dark cloth from his jacket pocket, wrapped the gun in it, and stowed it back into the pocket.

He joined the other guardsman, who was leading Madeleine away.

Commander Cook stayed in place, holding Doolittle's hand. He felt her strong grip enfold his hand. *That feels nice*, he thought. He heard Madeleine's cries get more and more faint, and he was vaguely aware that the guardsmen were taking her someplace.

"You okay, Doc?" Commander Cook continued to hold onto his hand, peering closely into his eyes. She said softly, "Everything's okay now, Doc. It's gonna be alright."

Doolittle nodded. But then he shook his head. He just wasn't sure of anything, right now.

Cook inhaled then exhaled, as if showing him how to do it. "Take a deep breath, Doc. See?" She did it again. "In. Out. See?"

He followed her lead. It did make him feel a little better. Like maybe he wasn't going to fall down.

"Good," she said, "That's good."

Still holding his hand, she helped him turn around, and walked him back towards the main building, where his pickup truck was parked. She led him to it, and then helped him sit down on the curb next to it. She let go of his hand, and sat down next to him, her short legs stretched out in front of her.

They sat side by side in silence for a while.

"Doc?" she asked.

He turned and looked at her.

"Did you know you just saved my life?"

He just stared at her.

She nodded, "You did. And I think you're in shock."

He blinked. Then nodded.

"So," she said, patting his knee with her broad hand. "We're just going to sit here, okay? For as long as it takes."

He said very quietly, "Okay then."

Chapter 24 – Miller Time

A week later, on Saturday afternoon, Doolittle parked his pickup in the gravel spot against the side of the weathered gray beach house. He reached over to the passenger seat, and grabbed the brown paper sack with his right hand.

He locked the truck then followed the rock path from the parking spot around the front of the house. He could hear the boom of the waves beyond the grassy knoll to his left. He climbed the steps to the broad porch, and knocked on the glass front door. When he saw the woman approach from the other side of the glass, he held the paper sack up chest high, and pointed at it with his left hand, grinning cheesily.

She opened the door, smiling up at him, "Doc."

"Commander," he said, and followed her beckoning arm into the house.

He handed over the sack, and she put it on the kitchen counter, opened it, and pulled out the sixpack of beer. Drops of water sweated down the sides of the bottles.

"Miller?" she said, smiling. "Seriously?"

He shrugged, "It was my dad's favorite. I can still hear him at night, after work: 'It's Mill-ah Time!'"

"Miller is just fine," she said, extracting two bottles out of the cardboard holder with one hand, picking up an opener with the other, and motioning towards the front door. "Shall we sit outside?"

"Sure," he said, and opened the door for her. She walked out onto the bleached wooden deck, and he followed her. She sat down in a wood Adirondack chair, and gestured him towards the other one. He sat, while she opened the bottles, then handed him one.

"Cheers," she said, and took a long drink from the bottle.

He did the same, then wiped his mouth with the back of his hand.

"That's good stuff," she said, leaning back in her chair.

"Only the best," he replied. He lifted the bottle slightly, "Commander."

She took another drink, then smiled. "Don't you think it's time you called me by my first name, Doc?"

He sipped his beer.

"It's Sandra. Sandy." She smiled, "I am pretty sure when you save somebody's life, you earn the right to call her by name."

He exhaled. "Okay, Command…I mean, Sandy. It's a deal."

She nodded, then placed her bottle on the wide arm-rest of the chair. She looked towards the ocean. Doolittle looked as well, and from here, you could just see the foamy tops of the waves over the stretch of sand dunes.

"It's nice here," he said.

"Yep. Susan inherited this place from her mom and dad. I moved in with her almost 20 years ago now."

Doolittle nodded, and took another sip.

"I like it a lot better when she's here. After she gets home from her seminar in Portland, how about you come back out and join us for dinner?"

He scratched the side of his neck, then said, "Sure."

"I make some mean Garlic Prawns," she smiled. "And Susan's grilled veggies are to die for."

"Sounds excellent," he said.

"It's a date then," she said.

"So, Command…I mean, Sandy. Can I ask you some questions?"

She leaned forward, holding the beer bottle on her exposed knee. He noted how different and less intimidating she looked barefoot, in her Bermuda shorts and Hawaiian shirt covered with pastel flowers. He scanned quickly from her spiky short hair, her wide shoulders to her big leg muscles. He noticed the tattoo on her right calf that read 'Susan' in calligraphy, with two intertwined dolphins. *I wonder if anybody at the station ever gets to see that?* he thought.

"Of course," she said. "Fire away."

"So, the guy I shot..." he hesitated.

"The captain, yes. He was Madeleine's brother."

"Okay, yeah. I'm still pretty foggy about some details."

She continued, "Well, at first it confused us, too. We expected him to be part of the mob, maybe Russian, you know, higher up. But he just ran the operation. Joe McCann, a regular guy from Port Townsend, Washington."

"I see," he said.

"Madeleine was his kid sister. From what we can piece together, they were raised without a mother, by a pretty hard core father. He had them stealing and poaching from a young age. I guess it was just normal to them, to make a living by crime."

"Sad," he said, taking another sip.

She nodded, "Yep. But Madeleine was smart. Got herself a scholarship to an ivy league school, planned to go to law school so she could keep Joe out of trouble. But then the Treasury Department came calling, and she saw an even better way to support her big brother."

"Wow." Doolittle placed his nearly empty bottle on the glass top of the driftwood coffee table between them. "Sounds like a sweet scheme."

"Yep," she agreed. "When the Secret Service thwarted Joe's operation in Port Angeles, Madeleine saw her opening. She had herself assigned to southwest Washington, and kept it quiet from both the Service and her own department."

"And how did she get him off that boat, without the rest of the agents seeing him?"

"From what she admitted during the debrief to her handler at Treasury, she and her brother had a back-up plan. He would hide in a specified spot, so she could pick her moment and get him off safely."

"Huh, crazy." Doolittle shook his head. "Can I ask you one more thing?"

She nodded, "Sure."

"How did Madeleine's own raft get shot up by the syndicate? I mean, how would her own brother let that happen?"

She shrugged, lifting her beer towards him, "I guess bad guys make mistakes, too." She took a sip, then continued, "Maybe Joe knew she was on their side, but some of his crew didn't? I guess we'll never know."

"And if I hadn't found her, oh man, it kind of makes my head spin."

She leaned towards him and patted him on his knee. "If you hadn't found her, Doc, and gotten pulled into all this, I'd probably be dead. And Tomás might have died, as well."

He nodded. "I guess."

"No guessing about it." She leaned back again in her chair. "You got skills, man, whether you like it or not. And I will forever be grateful."

"Hmm," Doolittle looked again at the waves, "My old partner Sam would laugh. He always said I was a 'lover not a fighter.'"

She followed his gaze, and watched the waves. "Well, I, for one, am sure glad that Sam was one hundred percent wrong."

On his way home, Doolittle parked in the side lot at the Little Store. When he walked through the front door, the door buzzer alerted Flora to his presence.

She looked up at him over the top of the counter and grinned. "Doc! How the heck are you?"

He smiled and bent to pick up a shopping basket. "Fine, I'm fine, Flora. You are you and Butch?"

He had no sooner said Butch's name than the giant man emerged from the back room. His voice boomed, "Well if it isn't my old friend Doc!"

Doolittle stood still and felt the friendliness roll over him.

"I was just thinking about you, Doc!" Butch limped towards him, holding onto the counter. "You're just the guy I wanted to see!"

"That so?" Doolittle answered. "How come?"

"Well," Butch squinted over at Flora, and she squinted back at him. "We got a call from that son of our old friend Mac this morning."

Wait for it, Doolittle thought. *Wonder what he's selling.*

Butch continued, "He wants to sell your cabin."

"What?" Doolittle felt the shopping basket get suddenly heavy in his hand. "Seriously?"

"Wait, wait," Butch held out his one good hand, reassuringly. "He said he wants to offer it to you first, Doc!"

Doolittle felt relief wash over him. He exhaled, then smiled. He didn't even ask the price. He looked at them both—down at Flora's upturned smiling face and up at Butch's towering grin.

"Okay then. Well, please tell him heck yes," he smiled. "I'm not going anywhere."

Made in the USA
Monee, IL
19 May 2023

33491639R00116